ONE STEP AFTER ANOTHER

THE AFTER ANOTHER TRILOGY, BOOK 1

BETHANY-KRIS

Published by Bethany-Kris

www.bethanykris.com

ISBN 13: 978-1-989658-31-4

Editor: Elizabeth Peters

Cover Design © London Miller

National Sexual Assault Hotline: 800.656.HOPE (4673)
Chat Online: online.rainn.org

CONTENTS

1.

Luca

LUCA saw ghosts everywhere. He figured that was to be expected considering he'd spent the better part of his days for a half of a decade chasing one. Now, whenever he found something that he could connect to his past, even when doing the most mundane things, he couldn't help but see the ghosts of what used to be.

But seeing what used to be often led Luca down the road of wondering what could have been as well. Very few good things came from *what ifs*; the past couldn't be changed, after all. Only the present and future. Chasing ghosts had also taught him that fact. A blessing and a curse.

"Sue the assholes for malpractice," the guy to Luca's left at the bar said to his friend in a suit. Well, they were both in suits. As was every other man in the bar and the connected ballroom of the hotel. Suit number one continued his chat with his friend, sipping on top-shelf bourbon, clearly knowing *nothing* about the law when he muttered around the rim of his glass, "Kid catches a virus while in the hospital unrelated to the illness they were admitted for. Sounds like something the hospital should have to answer for."

"That's what I said—"

"But not something you can *sue* for," Luca spoke up, drawing the attention of the two men to where he sat on a barstool. "Not rationally, anyway. The virus would have needed to cause significant harm to the kid. Medically or otherwise. It didn't—you said it yourself. Catching a virus because somebody coughed too close to him and didn't wash their hands doesn't fall under gross negligence. He had a few extra days in the hospital. Missed a test and a game. Another round of antibiotics and he was out of there. Big deal. You'll pay more for the lawyer and court costs than you would if you paid the original hospital bill. Waste of time."

Placing his lowball glass to the bar top, he pushed it closer to the other side for the bartender to pick up on his way by. One drink. That's all he afforded himself when he was working. Which was something he had to get back to, the entire reason he was there at the hotel during a political fundraiser, and he didn't really have time to entertain further distractions.

"Who the hell are you?" suit number two with the receding hairline and the wrong legal opinion asked.

At the same time, the guy's friend asked, "How would you know?"

1

Luca pointed at the first man, replying, "Me? I'm nobody." Then, to the other man, he added, "Five years of law school. But an ounce of common sense and all those forms the hospitals make you sign upon admittance that waives liability for almost everything *except* actual medical malpractice would have told you that. You know, had you taken the time to read them. Nobody does, do they?"

And saved Luca the trouble. Sometimes, he liked being an asshole, though. No real reason. At least it helped pass the time. The time was now up.

Standing from the stool, Luca reached for the blazer he had set on the empty stool on his other side. Usually, he preferred leather and a hoodie over a suit and tie, but there was no way in hell he was getting into the fundraiser looking like any other fuck who walked in off the street.

"Should still sue the bastards," muttered the one man. "What do you got to lose, Greg?"

Luca shrugged on his blazer. "Hell, his money to waste. I suppose if he's got enough money to be here—five-thousand dollars a plate for this event, right?—then he's got the cash to blow on frivolous lawsuits that clog up the justice system. But hey, whatever gets you off. I'm not one to judge."

"Excuse—"

Luca didn't bother to linger long enough to hear whatever bullshit the guy planned to say, and the buzzing in his pocket gave him a reason to turn his back when he pulled the phone out and answered the call. He hadn't checked the caller ID, but the second he heard the voice on the speaker, he wished he had.

"Puzza here," Luca said.

"Son," Zeke greeted.

Not *unkindly*.

It also didn't have to be. Just hearing his father's voice was enough to put Luca on edge. Usually, because Zeke's kindness was almost always followed by the man's—

"Dinner at your mother's favorite spot tonight. Did you forget?" A second of silence followed before his father added lower, "Again."

Disappointment.

The kindness was simply respect, and it always came before the disappointment. How his father showed or voiced that disappointment varied, but the end result was still the same.

"I didn't forget. Work," Luca explained, moving away from the bar and into the crowd of people milling between there and the ballroom where the tables had been set up for the pay-for-play political bullshit that he wasn't there to entertain. *Yeah,* he bought a plate to get into the event, but that had little to do with his intention to vote or which party he planned to pull for in the upcoming election. "Something came up. I talked to Ma."

"But not me which meant I showed up to find you weren't there. I appreciate the effort to let Katya know you wouldn't be joining us, but less that you couldn't take thirty seconds to call me and give me a heads up."

"Why? Then, we couldn't have this pointless conversation, Dad. You know how much I like our back and forth when I'm on a job. It really puts me on my game."

"*Luca.*"

Shit.

It didn't matter that he was a thirty-year-old man out on his own who answered to no one but himself—most of the time—his father came from a different generation. Really, an entirely opposite world. One that demanded respect at every turn and that he wanted Luca to join by jumping in with both feet and open arms.

The world of *Mafiosi*, that was.

Cosa Nostra.

A long time ago, Luca planned to do exactly that. Join the family business. Follow in his father's footsteps to hold one of the highest seats in the Donati criminal *famiglia*. Then life got in the way.

The past.

Those *ghosts.*

"Sorry," he told his father. The respect of the matter; Zeke expected it and even if he did see Luca's lack of involvement in the mafia as a failure on his part, he was still his father's son. "But something came up. I couldn't put it aside. Might be my only chance to—"

"Find whatever you're chasing this week," his father said, his tone rough with annoyance. "Who are you working for this time? Or is the better question, what are you looking for?"

"Wrong questions, right words. *Who* am I looking for," Luca returned, "and I'm not at liberty to say."

Well, he *was.*

Could.

But he didn't because Nazio Donati—the man who he answered to for this specific job—didn't like having someone else's nose in his business. Regardless of his status as a made man in the mafia alongside Luca's father. Considering Naz was also Luca's best friend—and married to Luca's little sister, Rosalynn—and this was a job he had been unable to complete since he started tracking things and people years ago … well, what did it matter?

His father wouldn't care. It wasn't what Zeke wanted Luca to be doing, and that's really what it all boiled down to at the end of the day.

He also no longer had time to fuck around. The beep of his other phone—an untraceable burner he replaced every two weeks just to be safe—said his night was just about to get started.

"I'll call you back," Luca said.

"No, you won't."

"Okay, I won't. I will, however, make it up to Ma for missing dinner tonight. That can either satisfy you or not. I don't have the time or the give a damn to keep going back and forth with you about it right now."

"Luca—"

"Sorry for the attitude. *Again.*"

Except he wasn't.

At all.

Luca didn't bother with an appropriate goodbye. His father should have figured out how the phone call was going to end two minutes ago when they first started it, anyway. Replacing the one phone with the other in his pocket, Luca checked the most recent message.

Confirmation of sighting—cameras at the front caught an arrival of someone matching your Penny's description. Matches the old picture I have. Except the hair. It's black.

Black hair.

Probably a wig.

Luca replied, *Keep watching the cams. Let me know direction and/or floors.*

The next response came fast, before Luca could even turn the corner to get a decent view of the front entrance to the hotel.

Got it, Keys wrote. A black hat hacker named *Keys,* funnily enough. Like computer keys. As if that wasn't ironic at all. He kept the guy on call for quick jobs, and the occasional deep dive search of the dark web when Luca couldn't find what he needed on his own.

Tonight, he had the guy working his magic on the hotel's security system because a bead he had a source from months ago suggested his current *active* mark would show up at the hotel fundraiser after arriving back from a trip overseas.

Why, he didn't know. Where had she been—another question he couldn't answer. There were too many unknowns when it came to the ghost he'd been tracking for five *long* years. She was the entire reason he had stumbled into his current profession, actually.

Every time someone left a clue or a lead popped up, it was scrubbed away as fast as it appeared. Like it hadn't existed in the first place.

But wasn't that the point of ghosts?

They *didn't* exist.

They couldn't be seen.

Thing was—Penny Dunsworth wasn't a ghost. Living, breathing … heart beating. She was just as real as him or anyone else in the world. She was simply harder to find.

Luca knew her once. So had his friends ... family. The young woman they invited into their world and life, someone they bent over backward to help and protect, until she just up and disappeared one day.

For no reason.

With no trace.

They wanted to know why—or rather, Luca's friend did. Nazio and his wife couldn't accept that Penny left on her own. Not considering her history and what led up to her eventual disappearance. Luca wasn't inclined to believe it either which was why he kept looking.

Even when Penny, a ghost of what they knew her to be, made it particularly hard. She couldn't hide everything. Or the people she worked for couldn't, anyway. Which was how he found himself at the hotel. And her supposed connection to an organization based in Nevada known only as The League.

He couldn't confirm it. That was the kind of the point, he suspected. Not that it stopped him.

Finding the unfindable certainly made Luca a good living, and it kept his head above water. It gave him something to do when his leads on Penny ran dry, and he had to wait for something else to pop up.

But that flash of pin-straight black hair under a large brimmed hat just beyond the entrance of the hotel said his lead on her was currently red-hot. In five years, the closest he had ever been to coming face to face with Penny Dunsworth had been ... never. He was always minutes too late, or entirely off the mark.

He wasn't about to let this chance slip through his fingers. He owed it to his friends to find the woman they had taken in as one of their own. So they could finally know *why.*

Right?

Time to get to work.

2.

"MISS Carter, whenever you're ready."

Regardless of how many times Penny Dunsworth used aliases—*many* times over her five years as an assassin working for The League—she had never really become accustomed to the revolving door of identities. It was part of the job. Expected, even. Yet, hearing another name that wasn't hers still took Penny a second to answer.

"Thank you," she told the driver currently holding the right side, rear passenger door open. "We won't need further help, or the car."

"I was told to be here at twelve to—"

"Excuse me," Penny said, stepping out of the vehicle and turning her back to the man as she grabbed the edge of the car door. It forced the driver to move, but also allowed the other passenger in the rear seat to exit as well. "Hurry. We're not drawing attention here, Delilah. Remember?"

Compared to Penny's form-fitted black gown, matching hat—that was better suited for the beach than the formal dinner and event happening a few doors away inside the Manhattan hotel—Delilah's white get-up was quite a sight as she left the vehicle. Well, Delilah wasn't her real name, but it was what her papers said, and Marise liked the option when Dare handed over the five different identifications for the job. Choices were always good.

Today, Marise was Delilah. Penny was Georgina. And none of it was true.

The skirt of Marise's white gown, made up of layers of chiffon, ruffled in the wind but not much. The silk cloak with the large hood that kept her blonde hair and most of her face hidden from any view up above—camera angles, mostly—kept the loose layers of the gown from blowing wildly.

Side by side on the street, Penny and Marise probably appeared to be total opposites. She towered over the girl's four and a half feet by a foot and half in her patent leather pumps. Their gowns were a contrast in both color and style. Even their hair—Marise with blonde curls, and Penny in her pin-straight black wig—couldn't be more different.

And yet despite those obvious physical differences, if anyone asked, the story was simple—Penny was Marise's mother. Or … the identities they had taken on were a mother and daughter pair, for that matter.

On the surface, anyway.

Beneath that, well, things were a lot darker. As was usually the way in their business. A person couldn't play with monsters and never come face to face with one, after all. In all her twenty-three years, it was one lesson Penny almost wished she had never learned. Thing was, if she hadn't learned it, then she wouldn't be who she was now.

"Miss Carter, this way, please," said the man in a three-piece black suit with coiled wire hanging down from the comm in his ear. He held open the front door of the hotel while another man, dressed similarly, stood a foot back in the entryway. Definitely not hotel security—more likely part of the team for the father of the man Penny would soon be visiting upstairs in a suite.

Penny smiled. "Absolutely. Delilah, follow me."

Her partner on the job said nothing but didn't hesitate to trail behind Penny who followed the two men dressed in black. The men didn't speak to each other, or the women walking only two feet behind. Or to any of the many people milling about in the large entry of the upscale hotel. Music and laughter filtered in through the open doorways of the bar and ballroom decorated in lengthy, sheer drapes.

Penny took all of it in. And barely even moved her head to do it.

Besides, it wasn't like she hadn't been to a dozen of these kinds of events when she was younger. A wealthy family, too much privilege and power ... of course, she had been dressed up and dragged to things exactly like this just because it was good for their last name to be tied to it all.

Not that she cared to think about it.

She never did.

Liar, her mind hissed as a hundred memories passed through her brain, making her heart beat harder and her chest tight. She was a liar because she thought about it too much.

Penny had just become better at hiding it. The League helped with that. Not that she was willing to admit the training they put her through had helped beyond anything more than teaching her how to kill another human in fifty different ways.

"Step inside," the man to the left said as he and his partner came to a stop near the elevators. Only one was already open and waiting.

Penny moved into the open elevator at the far right of a bank of four. Marise didn't need to be told to follow, nor did she raise her head enough to allow the cameras outside or inside the elevator to catch more than a shadow or the curve of her lips. The same way Penny's hat kept her face from view despite it not really going with the outfit.

Win some, lose some.

"Floor eight, right?" Penny asked, smiling at the suits waiting outside.

"Floor eight. Suite eight-oh-one."

She knew that, too.

At least the assholes could feel like they were really doing something more than just delivering a man's fetish.

Penny hit the button for the appropriate floor and waited until the door closed before she hit another. Two floors lower than the eighth. "You'll be fine—just get the hell out of here and make sure they don't see you leave, huh?"

Marise passed her a look. "What if he has someone waiting up there? Another one of those assholes in a suit—one with a *gun*?"

That was cute.

Funny, even.

She could do these jobs alone except for when she couldn't and needed a decoy. Say like another assassin who, when dressed up a certain way looked younger than she was. As far as Penny knew, Marise was somewhere in the range of eighteen years or so. About the same age Penny had been when she walked into The League five years earlier with a black folder in hand and no idea what would come next.

Except for tonight.

Because tonight, Marise—or *Delilah*—wasn't supposed to look her age at all.

"Get off on the sixth floor," Penny said. "No one will be waiting up there with him. They never have anyone. The entire point of what they do is the less who know, the better."

Marise didn't argue. She also got off the elevator on the sixth floor.

The rest, Penny could do alone.

Besides, she liked it that way.

• • •

Elijah Edward Smithenson the III.

Yes, his lineage was as arrogant as his name suggested. He came from a long line of politicians. His great-grandfather, grandfather, and so on. The son of a current prominent democratic senator who was planning a run for president in the coming election. Or that was the rumor amongst the political crowd.

People who knew what they were talking about.

Apparently.

Elijah himself was being looked at to follow in his father's footsteps seeing as how the last state election won him the mayor's seat. A position his father, the second, first won that started his overall career in the political sphere.

On the outside, the man seemed like he had everything he wanted. Wealth. Prestige. Power.

And none of that meant *anything* to Penny except for the fact that he ran in the same circles as people she had been hunting for years. One member of the elusive Elite. One more for her to kill.

Or that was the plan.

Currently.

Room 801 faced a long hallway with no guards keeping watch as Penny stepped out of the elevator. The hallways to the right and left of the bank of elevators where she stepped out were also empty. One led to what looked like two more suites. The other ended at an exit stairwell.

Penny headed for suite 801.

She didn't bother to knock but instead simply opened the door and entered the hotel room as was previously agreed upon. No locked doors— nothing and no one would see Elijah come and willingly greet and invite in a visually *young* girl and her older handler inside his room.

The filthy rich could get whatever they wanted; whenever they wanted it. And sometimes, on nights when everyone was distracted around them— like Elijah's father's fundraiser dinner downstairs—and they had time to celebrate, they were known and prone to indulging their desires.

Illegal, immoral, or otherwise.

And sloppy about it, too.

Which was why Penny showed up with a girl who wasn't the age Elijah wanted but also wasn't going anywhere near his hotel room despite the high price he paid to make sure she did exactly that. Maybe his people—or him—hadn't been able to get a hold of one of his regular trafficked girls through the normal methods but either way …

His vice was her weakness to exploit.

Penny didn't mind at all.

"Mr. Smithenson?" Penny called when the hotel door clicked shut behind her. "Your delivery is here and ready for your attention."

"Just a sec," came the reply.

From a room across the large space; probably the master bedroom in the space. A quiet, dimly lit hotel room stared back at her as she pulled the nine-millimeter from the bag that the men in suits downstairs hadn't even bothered to check.

So fucking sloppy.

It was kind of sad, really.

"A million dollars earned to smile and eat dinner. Two hundred guests at five thousand dollars a plate. I can do the math … not a bad night for a politician raising funds for his next run," Penny said, screwing in the silencer she had taken from the bag.

"Oh, that's before the donations are added into the—"

Penny glanced up when Elijah's words cut off. She took in many things at once. The suite was about as fancy, large, and expensive as she expected. Luxurious rugs. Rich tapestries. Ornate lighting overhead and furniture that was appropriately *stuffy* but also old. Nothing that interested her.

Except for the man who had come to stand in the doorway across the room. He was already prepped to party. Dress shirt unbuttoned; slacks undone and showcasing the band of his briefs. A glass of something amber colored in his left hand.

Maybe it was the shock of seeing only one woman—and no little girl—standing there or it could have been the gun in her hand that stunned him into silence.

"What the fuck are—"

"Nighty night," Penny said, not wasting time.

She couldn't. Not when she had to be in and out of the hotel in fifteen minutes or less.

Before Elijah could react—run, scream or otherwise—Penny did what she was there to do. Fifty hours of target practice with weapons meant she didn't miss a shot. Shit, she didn't unholster a weapon unless she intended to fire it, and she didn't shoot unless she meant for it to hit the target in front of her.

That was her training. She couldn't forget it.

It was a single shot. Hit Elijah between the eyes.

Penny had already tucked the weapon back away into her bag and stepped further away from the door before the dead man's body hit the carpeted floor with a dull thud. Such a morbid, but indifferent, sound for the end of a life.

Not that this particular life mattered.

If given the choice, Penny would have taken a lot more time with the kill. Really made it worth her time to be there in the first place while Elijah suffered as she was sure he'd made *many* others suffer. People like her ... even if he hadn't hurt her.

Monsters just like him did before. Could she be blamed for wanting to play with her kills in that case?

She didn't bother to give the corpse a second glance before stepping over it to finish the rest of her job. Killing Elijah was certainly on the list but gathering anything that would lead to anyone else—*higher*, more powerful people—doing even worse things than him ... well, that was a better deal.

Two birds, one stone.

Penny liked that. The people she worked for preferred efficiency, too.

She found his laptop and phone in the bedroom. And a USB drive in the pocket of a pair of pants hanging in the back of the closet. All in all, the kill and collection took less than five minutes.

That was a new record.

3.

"EIGHTH floor."

"You're sure?" Luca asked.

"How much are you paying me again?"

Luca came up the stairs two at a time. "What does that have to do with—"

"Two grand," Keys muttered on the phone. "You're paying me two grand for—at most—an hour's worth of work here. I'm doing said work while having a drink down the street. Easy work. You pay well, on time, the money's good, and you don't cause me problems otherwise. I tend to like clients who work with me the way you do. It makes for a good business relationship, you know what I mean? I'm not about to fuck that up, Luca. Your chick in the big black hat came off the elevator on the *eighth* floor. Anything else?"

"No cameras on the hallway on that floor?"

"Only outside the elevators. Not with a very wide view, either."

"And she hasn't come back—"

"Not to get on the elevators or to go in a different direction. She's still there and from the floorplans I checked out ahead of time of the hotel, the direction she went only leads to a technical dead-end. A room. Eight-oh-one on that floor, to be precise. You want a text if she does get back in my line of sight on the cameras?"

"As soon as she does."

"Got it."

"Thanks, Keys."

"Just doing my job, man," the hacker replied.

Right.

A job that Luca would still have to pay for whether he managed to get the woman cornered this evening, or not. More money flushed down the toilet if the night didn't end to his benefit. Not that he was ever clear on what he should do when—or *if*—he managed to catch Penny.

Bring her home, Naz had once told him.

I just want to know what happened, Roz said to Luca once when he asked his sister. *I want to know if we did something ... or didn't.*

Penny Dunsworth wasn't like every other search and find job Luca had taken on over the years. Even if it was her very disappearance from their lives a half of a decade earlier that had been the catalyst to bring him into his current profession. For one, because he didn't usually work for friends and in this case, Naz was exactly that while calling all the shots regarding Penny ... and Luca's work in finding her. But more importantly, because there was always a clear motive and objective once he found whatever it was that was missing.

Naz's desire to bring Penny home to his wife and the rest of their people for the reasons why she just up and disappeared after her eighteenth birthday ... as if she would *stay*. Like five years hadn't passed and who knew what happened in between?

If this *was* Penny he was chasing, Luca seriously doubted she was the person she had been before she left their lives. And at twenty-three now, it wasn't like they could force her to remain with them or even get the answers *some* of them were so desperately seeking. That was before they factored in whatever else she was doing. Her *work* ... the connections she apparently had to a very dangerous organization.

None of it spelled good things.

But his friend asked.

His *best* friend.

So, what did it matter if Luca didn't have a clear motive or objective once he got his hands on Penny? Who cared if he didn't have the first clue what the plan was *once* he had her back? All Naz would care was that Penny was home—it would satisfy whatever compulsion he had to find her, and his wife's sadness that hadn't left the woman since she woke up to find the girl she loved and cared for was gone.

Right?

As for Luca ... well, shit.

He just wanted to make things right. Like he didn't blame himself for missing something years ago when he thought he had started to make friends with a young woman who had clearly been planning to leave long before she ever came into his friends' custody.

This was why Luca didn't take jobs from friends or family. Emotions got in the way and clouded his judgment and rationale. Love made them all do stupid things because if in five years Penny hadn't returned, not even bothered with a *phone call*, then clearly, she didn't love them the way they had loved her.

There wasn't a single mark in his history that fucked him up the way Penny did. He wasn't sure if that was a good or bad thing only because his desire to catch her had become an obsession of sorts. One that wouldn't be satisfied until he had finally done his job.

Maybe it was the fact that in all his years tracking the ghost of Penny Dunsworth, never once had he been close enough to breathe the same air as her. He'd never been just *seconds* behind her. It was all he could focus on.

All he knew.

It was the only thing racing through his mind when he passed a young girl dressed in a white, flowy gown. Not unusual considering the formal event downstairs even if she did look too young to be wandering a very large hotel on her own. It was a little strange to him that she didn't just take the elevator but instead the emergency stairwell. He also didn't have time to stop and question her.

Her gaze met his as they side-stepped one another one in the stairwell, and their stares lingered for the length of time it took to pass by. Something about her was familiar. He didn't know *what.*

He only cared about catching Penny.

That was the problem.

• • •

Luca hadn't expected to find a guard wearing a black suit with a wire comm hanging from his ear waiting outside the exit door inside the stairwell on the eighth floor. Only because Keys hadn't mentioned seeing one on the cameras. That would have been an important detail to know.

Helpful, and all.

He wondered if the guy had seen Penny head to room 801 earlier or if she had noticed him. Either way … it didn't matter because now he was in *Luca's* way.

Luca plastered on a fake smile, hoping to distract and get past the guy without a problem. The suit eyed him when he leaned sideways to glance beyond the glass window of the exit door and pointed at the bank of elevators he could see. "Got lost—place is crazy tonight. Wouldn't have booked the whole week had I known there was going to be a political event. Don't mix pleasure with politics, you know? Will that elevator take me—"

"Only Smithenson family on this floor," the guy said, offering nothing else.

In fact, he altogether turned his gaze away from Luca. That was fine. It allowed him to size up the guard while he considered what the man said.

What was Penny doing—or who was she visiting—on the floor where the Smithenson family was staying in the hotel? The same political family currently raising funds downstairs from wealthy donors.

The guard was two inches shorter than Luca's six-foot-two. But the guy also had probably forty pounds of muscle on Luca's fit one-ninety-nine. So, he had a bit of height on his side, and the occasional kickboxing training that had become more and more infrequent over the years as he focused on his job might help but …

"Really," Luca said, taking a step forward and reaching for the door. "I'll only take the elevator back down to my fl—"

Luca didn't even reach the doorknob or finish his sentence before the guy grabbed his wrist and squeezed hard enough to make him flinch. *Not* that he did so, or showed his irritation.

"I said no entrance to this floor, asshole. And how the fuck are you getting *lost* when you've had a room booked for the week, anyway?"

He smirked.

Good catch.

Maybe the guy wasn't just meat shoved into a suit. Not that it was going to do him any good at the moment. Luca had been willing to forgo violence thirty seconds ago had he been able to get past the man but now …

Too bad.

"I lied," Luca said frankly.

And with a shrug.

Just because.

Honesty *was* the best policy, wasn't it? Especially in cases where it gave Luca the leverage of shock.

The guard's head snapped to the side, his gaze nailing into Luca, but it was already too late. He used his free arm to lift fast and hard, and his elbow hit the intended target. The nose of the guard which broke on impact. *And* stunned the guy just long enough for Luca to get his forearm against the man's throat as he pinned him to the wall.

Forty *unfortunate* seconds later, because the man bled all over Luca's arm, and he let the asshole fall to the floor before stepping over the unconscious body. Chances were, by the time he woke up, Luca would already be gone from the hotel.

Hopefully with Penny. Even if he hadn't figured out how to make that happen yet. Shit, if all else failed, he would just go the same route for Penny that he'd gone for the guard. Why not?

Luca reached for the doorknob at the same time something down the hall beyond the door caught his attention and froze him to the spot. A black hat, that was. And the long, white-blonde hair now peeking out from beneath the rim, falling over the delicate line of her shoulders in soft waves. Shoulders that were covered by the sleeves of a gown that went all the way down to her wrists.

Scars, he knew.

She must still cover those.

Had she been wearing a wig earlier?

It was the change in hair color that shocked him the most. Just for a second. Long enough to make Luca pause and wonder what the fuck he was supposed to do now. He'd never even been this close to her in all these years.

Penny.

She stopped in front of the elevator, reaching out to push the button to open the doors. The black gown she had worn for the evening—or job, whatever the fuck she was there for—was a tight number that hugged her curves and showed off how well she could pull them off.

The last time he saw her ... she was eighteen.

Barely a woman.

Barely fucking legal.

Practically a mouse in the way she had trouble talking to men, or women ... *anyone.* Back then, the Penny he met that his sister and best friend took in couldn't gain the courage to lift her head to meet someone's stare. She'd worn clothes that drowned any suggestion she was a female and regularly ran from the pain that chased her day and night.

He shouldn't know any of those things. It was part of the reason that made this *job* so goddamn complicated for Luca. And yet, he did.

It's why he paused.

Why he *stared.*

And why he couldn't stop staring.

He hadn't gotten a good glimpse of Penny when she came into the hotel downstairs. Hadn't gotten a peek at her in years beyond the occasional grainy security photo. He couldn't even guarantee the woman who came in downstairs had *been* Penny until this moment. With her profile in full view through the glass of the door, there was no question in his mind.

It was absolutely *her.* The mark he couldn't catch. The one he couldn't find.

Until now.

Penny.

Her heart-shaped face had thinned from the roundness of her youth, making her cheekbones sharper and her chin more angular. Those painted-red, full lips were not something he expected—he couldn't remember the younger her ever wearing make-up even if the rest of her pale skin still looked like porcelain glass. The ice-blue, wide doe-eyes were the exact same, though.

It was that second when Luca realized he'd been chasing an *idea* of Penny. The image he had imprinted into his memories of her—of the girl that his sister and best friend desperately wanted to find. Certainly not this grown woman who he had to do a double take of because he was a man who had never learned how to look away from a beautiful woman.

He'd been right.

That Penny was a ghost.

This woman was real and every part of Luca knew it. That was the problem, though. He *shouldn't* notice those things at all.

The black purse hanging off the corner off her elbow swung a bit when she stepped back and glanced upward. Maybe at the lights overtop the elevators. The groan from the man on the floor took Luca's attention away from the glass for only a second before it was right back on Penny down the hall.

She stepped forward when a ray of light shone across the carpeted floor. The elevator doors had opened. Like a fool, he'd been stuck staring at her instead of *moving* and was about to lose his one and only chance in five fucking years to catch her.

Luca yanked open the door at the same time Penny took another step. The noise of the heavy door had her glancing his way, recognition lighting up her eyes.

Then again, it could have also been him calling out, "*Penny.*"

4.

PEOPLE liked to say the past always catches up eventually. No matter how hard someone tried to leave it behind or how fast they ran away from it, it would eventually show right back up to laugh in someone's face.

Penny didn't think the sentiment was untrue … she had simply hoped that with enough time and distance, her past would stay where it belonged. It's what she worked for—what her handlers tried to make happen by keeping her out of North America as much as possible for the better part of her first three years working under The League as an assassin.

That way, everyone was safe.

Or so she was told.

All of that effort was totally blown to shit when Luca Puzza stepped inside the elevator after sticking his arm into the closing door to keep it from shutting completely. Given there were another five people in the space, a family guessing by the way they all chatted behind her, Penny did her best to keep from swearing out loud. She hadn't expected people to be on the elevator at all when the Smithenson floor wasn't available to other patrons of the hotel. But the elevator *would* open up to let people on from the Smithenson floor when it was carrying others from higher floors lower, she supposed. It was just her good luck that the elevator hadn't been empty coming down.

She didn't, however, hide the burning stare she leveled on Luca when he cocked a brow and grinned as he came to stand directly in front of her, and the elevator doors closed behind him. Effectively closing the two of them together in a small space.

Exactly what she needed to avoid. She'd hoped the door would close before he could reach it, maybe he'd make a run for the stairwell where he first came out of,

but he couldn't guarantee which floor she would exit on … giving her a better chance to get away.

She wasn't so lucky.

And didn't he look happy about it.

The handsome bastard.

Fuck.

It was those green-blue eyes of his—so intense and *familiar*—that threw her back in time. *Years.* So many years. Back to an entirely different world when she was a different person running from monsters instead of just hunting them down. To a family—who despite not being her own blood, had loved her, and taught her how to love—she had left behind.

It wasn't just her past Penny ran from but *everything* she left there, too. Her feelings and fears; her truths and lies.

Now, one of them was staring her right in the face. She might not have laid eyes on Luca in five years, but time meant nothing at that moment. Time stopped. Everything about his face was exactly the same from the chiseled cheekbones and strong jaw to the way his stare froze her in place from the heaviness that grew in her chest.

"Been a while," Luca said. "Hasn't it, Pen—"

"Don't."

He stopped talking.

She didn't say more.

The last thing she needed was this man saying her first name in an elevator full of witnesses after she had just murdered a man. Not that they knew it—or even Luca.

The family behind her kept talking.

Luca's lips twisted in a smile that made Penny's chest even heavier when he reached behind himself to push a button on the elevator as he asked, "Ground floor, then? You leaving? I'd like to come along. Have a word. Naz and Roz miss you."

Apparently, time meant nothing. That weight making her heart pound harder was the same thing she used to feel whenever this man smiled at her all those years ago. What a cruel, sad joke that even her foolish notions of a young woman would chase her into adulthood, too.

Her *crush*, that was.

On Luca.

Everything about Penny was different from how she used to be. She made sure of that. Her training helped. Her handlers *promised* it. It seemed that also wasn't the case because Luca could still make her tongue-tied at the worst possible time.

She hated how smug and gorgeous he looked when he moved to stand beside her, also putting his back to the chatting people in the elevator. She hated it even more that she noticed how well his suit fit him and that she could appreciate that fact when she could only remember one other time when he'd worn a suit in her presence.

Her eighteenth birthday.

The same night they kissed.

Her first *real* kiss.

If she cared to indulge *that* thought, then she knew damn well her mind wouldn't let her forget how it felt to have him kiss her. All because she asked; she had wanted nothing more than to be kissed simply because she wanted it. Something on her terms; born from her desires. With someone she trusted.

That someone had been *him*.

"Did you know about me?" Luca asked.

Penny didn't know what he meant for sure, but she had a damn good idea. "That you've been tracking me for years?"

"All these years, in fact."

Right.

Couldn't let that slide.

"Why do you think they make it so hard for you to catch up?"

Luca nodded, a glimmer of appreciation in his gaze that stayed nailed on her as though if he blinked, she might disappear. Hell, he wasn't exactly wrong. If he gave her the chance to get out of there without him on her tail, then she was absolutely going to take it.

She didn't have a choice.

Penny came and went.

She didn't leave a trace.

"You know I can't let you go tonight, right?" he asked.

She was only grateful for the fact that he kept his tone down, frankly. Too low for their guests to hear and below the shitty music playing through the speaker overhead. The speaker that was located right beside the blinking number that kept dropping with every floor they passed on their way down.

"Give me a day—or night, rather," Luca said. "Go see them. Naz and my sister, I mean. Explain what the fuck happened. What *did* happen?"

Penny didn't reply because she couldn't. What difference would it make to a man who had been chasing any and all breadcrumbs of her very existence for years? All on what, the off chance that he might be able to return her to people she had been forced to leave behind?

It wasn't like she could explain why.

They wouldn't *understand*.

Even she didn't.

Not completely.

Her gaze snapped up to the numbers overhead still counting down.

Five ... four ...

She needed a plan and *fast*. Chances were, her handlers from The League wouldn't be willing to let actual contact between her and Luca slide. Not when the entire point of her taking the offer to train and work as one of their assassins had rested upon the need of leaving everyone in her life behind. Beyond that, this could only cause more trouble for the actual *job*.

Another reason for the people above her to get rid of the issue altogether.

"I'm a bit confused," Luca murmured, sticking his hands in his pockets which was at least one thing she didn't have to worry about. Fewer appendages to fight back when she took him by surprise in another couple of floors, right? That was the only way to fix this situation by all accounts. She needed to make it out of here cleanly.

Or as clean as possible.

She didn't *want* to do that to Luca. At the same time, he really didn't give her a choice tonight. Any other night, had he accosted her—though she had no clue how he managed to track her this time, but they knew her working in the states would be dangerous—then she might have been able to do … *anything* else.

Indulge his conversation. Lie. *Run.*

Tonight, there was no option.

She *had* to get away.

Without him.

"Confused," he continued, tipping his head her way, "because clearly you have freedom. See, I have heard the rumors about the organization you work for. What they do—who you *are*. And in all this time, if you knew we were looking for you … why didn't you try to come back? Or call? Anything? Did you think the time you were with my sister and Naz meant *nothing* to them? To me? We lo—"

"Shut up," she snapped.

Her sharp hiss *did* quiet the people behind them. She could practically feel their gazes burning into the back of her head. Probably taking in the long-sleeved gown she wore and the color of her hair. Imprinting the image of her to their memory, so they could relay it later to police when the dead body was found upstairs, and the mysterious woman caught on camera coming and going from the eighth floor was connected.

Two and two always made four, after all.

Jesus.

Penny was really screwing this job up.

Not her usual style.

Luca sighed. "You're not even going to say a thing to—"

The elevator jumped when it came to the third floor. Rubber squeaked when the doors opened to the hotel's floor with the pool. The same floor that had been lit up on the elevator's switchboard from the second she stepped inside.

Had Luca been slightly less distracted by her and trying to get her to talk, then he might have noticed the same things she did. That the people behind them weren't exactly dressed for the party downstairs. That they all held towels. Even the light on the switchboard designating the floor they intended to get off on …

Where the pool was.

It told her a couple of things. She did have her opening to escape. This would end badly for Luca because he hadn't given her a choice. And his chance to find her tonight had happened so quickly that the man didn't even have time to properly check out the hotel in such a way that he would be aware of the pool on the third level.

The people moved forward, forcing Penny and Luca apart and creating a sea of five moving bodies that acted as a curtain for privacy between them. He didn't see her reach into the bag she had been carrying all night—the one that held the gun, the electronics she had taken from Elijah's room, her wig, and anything else she might need for the night.

Including a syringe full of a sedative that would work in less than six seconds once injected straight into the neck. The people didn't look back as they exited the elevator.

Luca didn't even see the needle coming.

"*Fuck*," he snarled when she hit him with the syringe, arm swinging for her but missing because she had already shoved down the plunger and yanked her arm back. His wild gaze swung on her, angry and betrayed. "What did you just—"

"Tell them I'm sorry," she whispered. "I always am."

She at least caught Luca before he hit the floor. She got out on the second level instead of the ground floor because it wouldn't exactly look good to come out on the ground section full of a busy entry with a body in the elevator.

Right?

The job came first. Everything else was second. That was Penny's life now.

It had to be or no one, including Luca, would like what came next.

5.

Luca

"SIR … sir, I'm going to need you to calm down, please. Can you follow the light? Look into the light and follow where it goes."

Luca didn't know that voice, who it belonged to, or why the person it belonged to was currently holding him down. It was never a good thing to wake up confused, disoriented, *and* immobile against something *hard*.

His mind raced to catch up; to fill in the blanks as something bright waved in front of his blurry vision. He didn't know where he was, how he got there, or why it all happened. The faceless man behind the light spoke again, or his mouth moved anyway, but Luca didn't understand a thing the guy was saying.

Or he just didn't care to.

If he could see, and breathe, despite the fuzzy line of sight and the cloudiness in his brain then that only meant one thing to him. He was *alive*. What did it matter what the asshole with the flashlight was trying to say to him?

The next time the white light swung past his eyes, Luca attempted to strike out to make sure the prick didn't shine it in his face again. But when his arm didn't do what he wanted, or rather, stopped completely within a couple of inches, he finally understood why his body and limbs weren't doing what they wanted.

Lifting his head slightly from the hard surface beneath him, he could see the restraints locked around his wrists and attached to the metal bars of a paramedic's gurney.

Fucking hell.

How did that happen?

The *click-click* of wheels had him jerking on the bed, but the paramedic didn't miss a beat, keeping up to the moving gurney like it wasn't a problem at all. Overhead, Luca saw the name of a hotel written in a fancy script.

Luca slammed his head back into the gurney as the paramedic asked, "You were found unconscious in the hotel's elevator—do you remember what happened at all? What is your name? The date?"

A new voice came from behind Luca's head. "Anything?"

"Nothing verbal," said the man with the flashlight that Luca was going to shove up his ass the first chance he could. "Pupils are reacting, though. He *can* hear me, but he's not responding otherwise. Vitals are stable either way."

"Room eight-oh-one," he heard someone else say. *Not* the guy attempting to make conversation with him or the one navigating the gurney. "Found a body. Also, a guard choked out in the stairwell, but the guy said he didn't remember a thing when they finally got him conscious and talking. My bet, this dude's about to say the same."

"This guy wasn't choked out," Luca's new friend barked back.

"You don't know—"

"Yes, I do. No bruises or anything to suggest that's what happened. Also, there's a needle prick in the side of his neck, and he's so out of it that he can barely lift his head for more than a couple of seconds at a time. *Drugged.*"

"We need to talk to him," the other guy said. "Witnesses say he was in the elevator with the woman we think is connected to the murdered man upstairs ... possibly even talking to her. Security footage is being pulled as we—"

"And you can talk to him, officer, as soon he is conscious *and* aware of his surroundings while stable. At the moment, he seems to be only two out of three of those things. We will see you at the hospital."

"But—"

"*At the hospital*," snapped the paramedic.

That was the last of the conversation between the cop and the medics. In the next second, the gurney bumped into something hard enough to rock Luca before he was lifted higher, and the wheels rolled along something that sounded like metal. He had a clear view of the officer waiting outside the ambulance and the doors that closed him out.

Everything was becoming a hell of a lot clearer to Luca even if he didn't plan on acting like it. He couldn't; not if he wanted to get out of this current situation without cuffs on his wrists. That much was obvious. He was also grateful that the identification he brought along for the night was fake so anything they took off his unconscious body wasn't going to lead them anywhere once he got to the hospital.

What bothered him more?

That he remembered what happened.

Everything.

In painfully clear detail.

Penny did this.

She did all of it.

But *why?*

• • •

23

"Mr … Kutner," the officer said, glancing down at the medical chart he'd taken from the edge of Luca's hospital bed to double-check for the name he clearly hadn't been able to remember. "That is your name, correct?" Not even close.

Luca shrugged where he stood beside the bed, already dressed in his clothes from the night before—minus the bloody blazer that no one had seemed to notice—and ready to leave. His ride would be arriving soon. He didn't plan on this conversation with the cop lasting any longer than it had to.

"That's what the file says," Luca replied. "And my ID."

"Right, right." Flipping over a paper on the chart, the cop *huh'd* under his breath before glancing up to meet Luca's stare. "Yikes, hope someone is coming to drive you home because the drug you got hit with last night … a horse tranquilizer, apparently. How much do you remember about—"

"Little to nothing. As I told the nurses and doctors and the last cop that came in here. He was a bigger asshole than you, though. Chose the right career because I don't think he would have made it as the doctor he pretended to be with a bedside manner like that."

The officer chuckled. "Some of us have interesting methods of interviewing."

"Or some of you just like to have fun."

"Or you're lying."

Luca didn't bother replying to that. What would be the point? He didn't intend to shoot himself in the foot … or stick it in his mouth, for that matter.

"See," the cop continued, still eyeing Luca for even the slightest sign of a lie, not that he would find it, "security footage tells us a lot about your movements *and* our mysterious woman's last night. What we're slightly more interested in than the fact you seemed to take the same stairwell where one of the Smithenson family's security detail was found unconscious is what we saw in the elevator."

"Which was?"

"You talked to her. She didn't talk back. What did you say?"

"Can't remember," Luca replied easily.

Or *lied* easily.

Depending on how one wanted to look at it.

"You seemed familiar. Like you knew her."

The cop who hadn't even bothered to introduce himself to Luca reached for a paper on top of a pile he had sat on the table at the end of the bed. Holding the one on the top up, it was a photo of Penny and Luca standing side by side in the elevator. It didn't show Penny's face—the wide brim of her hat hid that. Her white hair was visible, however, as was the way he clearly looked at her from the side with a grin that spoke of *interest.* Couldn't hide that.

The man was right.

Luca did recognize her—there was a familiarity in his actions. There was also something else he could use for his current situation. Another lie.

"Can't see her face there but you should have," Luca said, chuckling under his breath. "Chick was hot—fuck me for taking a shot."

The cop cleared his throat. "Clearly it didn't work. The bitch stuck you with a needle the first chance she could."

"Yeah, shitty luck, huh?" Then, Luca arched a brow. "Did you catch her face at all?"

"No," the man replied. "Well, Mr. Kutner, thank you for … your lack of help. We will be in touch should we think of anything else. And if you remember something else—"

"I'll be sure to call."

"I'm sure."

Yeah, Luca knew that tone. The cop couldn't say he was lying but thought he was; Luca wouldn't verify or deny and since everything they had on record about him currently was a lie … they weren't coming back. They couldn't.

Just before the cop walked out of the room, he turned back with a finger pointed at Luca like a loaded gun when he asked, "And how do you remember nothing except for the fact she was attractive?"

Luca said the first bullshit to come to his mind because at this point, what did it really matter? "Spent five grand last night to eat with a bunch of bastards, got lost in the hotel, didn't even get the meal I paid for, and I got knocked out by some woman you think murdered a man. The *only* good thing about my night was her face. You're surprised I remembered it?"

"A little, yeah."

The man didn't offer anything more before making his presence scarce. Luca made quick work of pulling out the blazer he'd stuffed in a dirty laundry bin. Either the medics and cops hadn't noticed the blood during his treatment and observation the night before, or they thought it was related to his injuries.

Or they foolishly overlooked it.

Either way, he wasn't leaving it behind and before noon, it would be burned or handed off to one of the many homeless in the city to use as needed. Whatever made it disappear. And with his walking papers from the hospital at the top of his chart, Luca was free to leave.

He didn't even make it out of the room, though. Nazio Donati strolled in seconds before he had gathered what remained of his personal items sitting on the nightstand beside the bed. His friend shut the door behind him and then closed the blinds to shut out any view from the outside through the windows.

"What the fuck happened?" Naz demanded.

"Nice to see you, too, man," Luca muttered.

"Sorry—you're okay, yeah?"

Luca lifted one shoulder. "Better than I was a few hours ago. Nearly got a tube shoved up my cock when they thought the drug would last longer. That shit was the only motivation I needed to stop pretending like I couldn't understand what was happening. That was also around the time the cops started coming into my room. What are you doing in here? They think my name is James Kutner … you won't help that."

"Right, *right* … the only good thing about *not* being a made man and working for the mafia is that your pretty black and white picture isn't on every official's corkboard in the city, I suppose. How long do you think you can get away with being someone else before they figure it out?"

"Not much longer. Which is why we need to get the hell out—"

"Fuck the cops. I got in here clean. And I left Roz in the car," Naz said, shifting from foot to foot and observing the room like something was going to jump out of the walls at him. His best friend had always hated hospitals ever since he flew across the world thinking the love of his life—Luca's sister—was sick. "Not like we needed *two* Donatis in this place milling around. Drawing attention, and all. Not sure she would have been able to control herself either considering she thinks you're in here dying."

"She does not."

"I told her you were fine. Telling Roz one thing and her knowing it is entirely different. Now we *are* wasting time with bullshit. What happened?"

Luca headed for the door, moving to pass Naz as he said, "You should have sent someone else to pick me up."

"Stop."

Naz's hand stopped Luca from grabbing the doorknob when it latched tightly to his wrist. His best friend met his gaze, the question burning there but not being spoken out loud. It didn't matter if he said it; Luca could see it and that was enough.

"I was working. Shit went bad."

"Was it *her*?" Naz asked.

Luca swallowed hard. "Naz—"

"I know, you don't like to get my hopes up. You don't want Roz to know unless you've got something firm. I also know you've had a lot of last-minute shit come up lately, your father is calling mine to bitch every other hour about it, *and* you didn't tell me what you were up to last night. *Was it Penny?*"

"I didn't know for sure until—"

Naz let out a hard breath. "That's the first time you've actually seen her, isn't it?"

"Yeah, but that makes sense considering everything I've found on her says they've been keeping her overseas for ... whatever she does. Work, I assume. Killing people. It's only been the last year or so that she's been back in this part of the world, and it's a lot harder to keep every trace of her scrubbed from existence when people here *see* her and can pass on the word, likely."

His friend's brow dipped. "*They?*"

"That's what you took from all I said?"

"Who are they?"

Luca chewed over his next words but only because he didn't want to step in shit somehow. Not with Naz, or elsewhere. Like the people who had Penny on their payroll. "An organization called The League."

The slight brightening of Naz's eyes told Luca that wasn't the first time his friend had heard that particular name. "Huh."

"You know of it?"

"Of it," Naz agreed quietly, "partly. They deal with assassins. The training and *selling* of them. Handling their creations for their buyers for a fee. And that alongside everything else I've heard about them is enough to tell me to stay the hell away because I don't want their problems."

"That's going to be tough to do if you want me to find and retrieve Penny Dunsworth, Naz. I'm almost positive she's one of them.

"*Almost* positive?"

"It's taken me five years to even lay eyes on her, man."

Naz's jaw tightened. "*And?*"

"And that tells me the people behind her—maybe back then but *definitely* right now—are every reason why it's taken me this long. What do you want me to do now? Where am I going from here? Either I back off because I have a new starting point that's too dangerous for you, or I keep searching. Which do you want?"

A shadow passed by the shaded windows, quieting the two men just long enough for whoever it was to continue past the hospital room.

"I promised my wife answers about Penny and what happened all those years ago," Naz said. "She blames herself ... she misses her. I want those answers, Luca. Don't *you?* Don't you want to know why she left—or who made her leave?"

Tell them I'm sorry, Penny had told him. As the drugs she shot into his neck kicked in, and she helped him to the floor, she had added softer, *I always am.*

"What if she doesn't want to give the answers to us, Naz?"

Because that was a real possibility.

6.

Penny

IVORY and sugar pine danced beneath Penny's fingertips. The notes that echoed from the keys she played reverberated through the empty, dimly lit room in a compound she hadn't visited in weeks. That was usually how it worked when she was sent out on a job.

"I know you're there," Penny said, never looking away from the white cement bricks that made up the wall where the piano faced. "And you know I hate it when you stand behind me like you intend to—"

"I'm not going to sneak up on you," Cree replied. "Just enjoying the music."

Penny rolled her eyes.

Cree would say that, the asshole. The fact was, her handler—one of two at the League whom she answered to—knew her better than anyone. And even though she was supposed to be upstairs briefing Dare, the other asshole in the whole handler equation of her life, on her latest job … the first place she visited when returning was never to him.

Of course, Cree knew.

He knew everything.

"I also know you just rolled your eyes," Cree added like he could read her mind.

Penny didn't even bother to glance over her shoulder. She didn't need to in order to see the image of the large Native man with his glossy black braid falling neatly over his shoulder. Those dark brown-black eyes of his, the same color as molasses, would watch her with an aura of intensity she had become accustomed to over the years. His stare could feel both cold but probing at the same time. The man only needed to look at any one of the assassins he helped train to know the things hidden inside their souls.

It was kind of … fucked up.

And freaky.

"Dare is waiting whenever you're ready," Cree said.

"I'm sure."

"And he'll wait for whenever you're done."

Yes, he would.

"Although, he would rather not wait in this case," the man added.

Everyone here had come to learn a long time ago that when it came to Penny, it was far easier to get what they wanted by allowing her what she *needed.*

Nevada was supposed to be home. The place she always came back to again and again—year after year. *Job after job.* That was the rules she agreed to when she signed up to be trained here. No matter how far away she was sent for her next assignment, she always ended up right back in the Nevada desert inside a building full of people with the same skills as her.

It was a home, of sorts. Homebase for The League, maybe. She much preferred the hotel room that her handlers kept on a tab for her to come and go as she pleased whenever she stayed longer than a day or more in the state before heading off on the next assignment.

For her, she had forgotten what home felt like a long time ago. Before dark rooms, water tanks, knife training, and learning how many ways to kill a person while also memorizing the most effective methods to create poisons from simple ingredients found in a home.

The League didn't take away the place she called home because she never had one even before she came here. She thought she did—once. Almost. Until the idea of having somewhere to call home meant causing the people who created it for her unimaginable pain.

It was a dangerous thing, *hope.* The one and only time she had allowed herself any kind of hope for her future it had been ripped away before she even knew what had happened. Partly by her own choice, if she were being honest.

Self-sabotage had long been one of Penny's favorite pastimes. Back when she still had daily suicidal ideations and a blade that allowed her to feel something other than pain with every cut against her pale skin.

But that time was gone.

And now here she was.

It wasn't lost on her that despite not being able to consider The League's compound home—or the hotel she used as an apartment when needed—that she did, in fact, find comfort here. Specifically, the music room deep within the belly of the complex that had only been created after Penny's arrival.

It just showed up one day.

She didn't go near it—didn't breathe within ten feet of it—for the first two years. After all, she had thought that coming to this place meant giving up every part of her that had come before. Including her promising career as a pianist.

Except someone had taught her that the piano always meant pain for her. She hadn't learned to play for her own peace of mind, or even because she loved the music.

Not until Naz and Roz.

And then The League … well, the piano became a solace in a very dark—

"Does playing when you're here still take you away from what it all is— can you pretend to be someone else?" Cree asked.

Penny sighed. "Not when someone talks over my shoulder."

"You've not even missed a note. I'm barely bothering you. Don't deflect. I don't indulge your sarcasm like everyone else does. Not when I see it for what it is. Another way to protect anyone from getting close enough to your sharp edges where—"

Her fingers slammed down hard on the keys, making deep notes clang through the room and stopping Cree from spouting anymore of his Yoda bullshit. He wouldn't be wrong. She also just didn't care to hear it.

Was that so wrong?

Penny swung around on the piano bench to stare at the towering, broad-shouldered man leaning in the doorway to ask, "Is there something you need? Something *other* than asking questions you already know the answers to?"

"Dare would like an update sooner rather than later."

"I'm on my way."

"He *did* appreciate that you sent over the electronics from the Elijah Smithenson job yesterday when you first arrived, but since you waited an entire day … *and* you're in here right now, I'm sure you see where I'm going here."

"Rushing things along?" she asked.

Cree shrugged. "Is what it is, kiddo."

Penny scowled at that title. One he'd called her since she first walked through the front doors of this hellish place. "I'm twenty-three."

"And I'm old enough to have gray instead of black hair, but these genes of mine are determined to keep me young. What is your point?"

"Since when does Dare get you to do his dirty work?" Penny flipped a hand toward the ceiling and the upper levels of the complex where she knew, without a doubt, Dare was currently watching their exchange on one of his many cameras. People couldn't change who they were—another thing The League taught her—they could only hide who they used to be. "He knows where to find me."

"You *are* deflecting," Cree murmured, "but this time, it's not about the piano. Just like the piano thing a minute ago wasn't about the piano, Penny. I get the feeling the job didn't go exactly as planned, you're likely aware that we know, and that's why you don't want to go upstairs."

A frown pulled at her lips.

He wasn't wrong.

Again.

"Well?" Cree asked.

She wished she had even a tenth of the percent of information about this man that he knew about her. Or even the guy upstairs. She didn't even know her handler's last names; only that they let her kill every monster they could find.

All she knew about Cree and Dare and this place they called home were the things they could do—to her, to people she cared about, and to the ones she hated more than anything.

Everyone had to make choices. She had made hers long ago. Which was why she left the piano bench and headed upstairs to brief Dare. Even if that was the last thing she wanted to do.

● ● ●

"Laptop was worthless," Dare said when Penny finished recapping the important details of her trip to New York and the hit on Elijah Smithenson. "As was his phone, but we expected that."

"And the USB drive?"

"You didn't find that little device anywhere near the computer, did you?"

"Nope."

"Filled with what you would expect for a man of his tastes," Dare informed with a dry inflection that said nothing he found on the drive shocked him. That was a sad fact about this entire world she had fallen into; the monsters were everywhere, and they did the most monstrous of things. Nothing was surprising. "All files were, of course, wiped of anything usable regarding metadata, but we'll see what our people can do with the videos and photos. Connect it back, if possible. I assume you don't want to see—"

"Would rather not," Penny interjected shortly. "I don't need visuals when I already have a whole memory bank of my own to get me through cold nights, thanks."

Beside her, Cree folded his arms over his chest but avoided looking her way. Still, he said quietly, "Have you considered you might be able to help those ch—"

"I *am* helping."

Cree let out a weighted exhale. Dare didn't miss a step and continued with his previous discussion like the exchange between Penny and his partner beside her didn't happen at all.

"We can safely assume if Mr. Smithenson was willing to go outside his usual connections within The Elite for his fix," Dare said, his back facing Penny while he observed the many security cameras keeping watch on the halls and rooms of the compound, "then perhaps other members will do the same in the coming months. That will make knocking out a few more of them easier than we'd hoped. This is a good thing."

"Did you consider it might only be because of recent events?" Penny asked.

Dare lifted his silk-covered shoulders. The sky-blue hue of his button-down was a stark contrast against the light of the screens in front of him. "Depends on what you mean."

"I think it's likely the only reason he did go outside of the group is that their members keep showing up dead. Do you think they haven't caught on yet that someone is hunting inside their group? It was bound to happen."

"We don't have proof of that."

"Yet," Penny muttered. "It is inevitable. We knew that when we moved on to the group in the states. I'm sure they know it, too."

Dare didn't reply.

He rarely did to her attitude.

"Either way," Dare added, "we continue like we have. *Carefully.* One step at a time. We don't move without purpose, and we don't hit without—"

"I know."

Finally, Dare turned on his heels his ice-cold stare burrowing holes into her stoic form across the room. "Anything else you want to fill me in on while you're here? Or should I pre-emptively lock all the doors leading to the music room, so you can play unbothered for the next two hours before you leave?"

"Does my playing bother you?"

Cree tipped his head her way. "*Penny.*"

She knew it didn't bother them.

They gave her the room.

"This entire conversation would go faster—and easier—if Dare just said what he wanted to say instead of trying to dance around it like I'll willingly offer it."

"Why won't you?" Dare asked.

Like Cree, her other handler was approaching a later age in his life. Gray had started to color his hair, though, and the lines on his face gave him a visual sense that he had learned many things in his life. But the same way Cree could just look at Penny and know things, so did Dare. She wasn't sure if that was because she wore her truths on her sleeve or if it was something else. Something about *them.*

Either way, she hated it.

"Because it wasn't an issue," Penny said.

"A man that has been tracking you for years finally catches up to you *while* you're on a job, causes a problem during the—"

"After, Dare. The hit was done."

"Fact remains. He *is* an issue."

"Luca Puzza is just a man who knows my face," Penny said firmly. "You're right, he's been chasing my trail for years, and this is the first time he got close. A stroke of luck, nothing more. It's not something we need to act on. I handled it. Get your people on the reason *why* he found me, and work to make sure that doesn't happen again. There's no reason to make it bigger than it is."

Dare's jaw tightened. A sure sign he was pissed.

And didn't believe her.

He shouldn't.

Not that Penny would willingly say that out loud. Seeing her past right in front of her eyes had been a frank reminder of things—and people—she had been running away from for years. That didn't mean she planned to do anything with the complication he posed.

"He could be a problem to the grander plan, especially now that you're slightly easier to track being in the states more often while we infiltrate and dismantle The Elite," Dare explained. "I'm giving you the option now to allow me to correct the problem before I make the choice on my own because you leave me nothing else to work with. You know the deal, Penny. To make this work, nothing else exists … nothing from your past, your present, or your future."

She understood.

All too well.

She also wouldn't give the okay for Dare to make a call that would effectively end any hope that Luca would live to see the end of the week simply because he was doing what he had always done. He was only trying to find her … she knew why, too.

Because people loved her. She was also here because she loved them.

It didn't seem fair to hurt those people again by removing someone else from their life just because it might make this plan of Dare's for The Elite a little harder to see through. That was not her problem; she just did the killing.

It's what they wanted.

"Are we done?" Penny asked.

Dare's gaze drifted to his partner at Penny's side with a glint she recognized. He wanted to push; to question and ask more but that had never been his MO with her. He liked Cree to do that dirty work for him … just like the show downstairs. It wasn't by accident that Cree knew exactly where to find Penny or that he was the only person within the large complex that had been able to reach the music room despite all the locked doors. No one got anywhere in this place without Dare allowing it to happen through his security system.

In that moment, Cree was silent.

He wouldn't indulge whatever Dare was silently asking. Maybe because he didn't care to or, perhaps, he agreed with Penny. It didn't matter to her if they left the conversation—and Luca—alone.

Dare gave her a pointed look. "Don't play any games, got it?"

"What game?" Penny widened her arms, adding, "Call me when you can tell me the next move I need to make. You know where to find me."

7.

Luca

LUCA had long become accustomed to chasing people down—his best friend included. Naz's need to keep moving from one thing to another was only a by-product of his heavy hand in the family business. The mafia always liked to keep a man on his feet and running.

Sometimes, it meant Luca couldn't get a meeting in with his friend at all. Other times, it just meant he had to fit one in whenever he could. Even if that time was during a family breakfast at a restaurant in Brooklyn when they weren't supposed to be talking any kind of business at all. Not that it ever mattered to him.

It did, however, matter to the man who demanded the breakfast between the Donati family and Luca's.

He figured …

Rules were meant, and *made*, to be broken.

Right?

Even if breaking it meant risking the wrath of the family boss currently sitting at the head of the table and eyeing Luca from his spot as he slid into the chair beside Naz's after entering the restaurant. Cross Donati was a lot of things. Luca had grown up calling the man his uncle even if he wasn't related by blood. One of his father's very best friends, he had learned to appreciate the softer, family side, of the mafia boss before anything else.

Then, life got in the way.

Business, too.

He was given an entirely different kind of perspective on the man Cross could be when the situation and time called for it as Luca grew older and started to dabble in the family business. And it was that lack of ignorance about Cross that kept Luca quiet as the man continued watching him instead of going back to his previous conversation with his wife, Catherine, at the end of the breakfast table.

He didn't mind breaking a rule. He simply didn't want to do it *brazenly*. Therein lied the difference. Or at least, it was a good enough one for Luca when it came to Cross. There were some men he knew better than to provoke.

Cross Donati was one of those.

"Good to see you showing your face this weekend," came the familiar voice of his father from the other side of the table. "I figured you would still be chasing after someone's—"

"Zeke."

The quiet murmur crawled down the table from the boss's seat to Luca's father's all the way at the end. It silenced everyone as it passed, his mother, sister, and best friend included. When Cross said *no business* at family functions—even if it was just a simple breakfast—then that was exactly what he meant. Regardless of who sat at the table.

Luca tipped his head to the side, smiling at his ma and then nodding to his father. "Hey to you, too, Dad."

Zeke's jaw tightened but that was the only sign of his irritation otherwise. "Busy week?"

Luca lifted his leather-covered shoulders, happy to be back in his staple black jacket and hoodie for the time being. Hopefully, he wouldn't need to slap on another suit and tie for a while if he was lucky. But one never knew what the future held, either. "Busy life, Papa."

"Right, right."

"Are we eating or what?" asked Cross from down the way. "I'm starved."

The confirmative noise from the other Puzzas and Donatis at the table sent the boss clapping his hands and calling for the servers. Another benefit of this restaurant—the Donatis owned it. Which meant whenever a recognizable face from the family came through the front door, the employees jumped through hoops to make sure everything was perfect.

Luca decided to put the flood of servers coming into the private dining section to his benefit while everyone else around him was distracted. The servers came in with a choice of breakfast foods on platters, stopped at every person with a choice in coffee, juice, or water, and did their job. Quiet chatter bounced from person to person.

He turned to his friend.

"Guess what I got?" he asked Naz.

Naz thanked the woman pouring his coffee and blocking the view of the boss down the way before asking Luca, "What? And make it quick, you know how my father gets when we discuss any kind of business at a dinner table with family present."

"A reporter …"

It had taken Luca an entire week after the hellish fundraiser dinner that went to complete shit to pull together a decent amount of information about what exactly went on … but he did it. There could be only one reason why Penny had been there that night—to murder the son of the prominent politician who had been busy shaking hands downstairs while his son got a bullet between his eyes eight floors up.

The real question was *why?*

Why did she do that? Why Elijah Smithsenson?

Why that night—when the spotlight on the Smithenson was shining brighter than ever as they rallied funds from wealthy donors?

Why, why, why.

He hated *whys*.

And since the dead couldn't talk—and neither could the ghost he hadn't been able to catch—and the media had been mum on the details about the murder otherwise, Luca was left with only a few options at his disposal. He needed as much information on the murder, and the political family, as he could get his hands on. Something there would lead him to the whys he didn't have answers for about Penny's involvement in the murder.

He was sure of it.

It was the only thing that happened in the hotel that night—she was *on* Elijah Smithenson's floor. The media's lack of discussion on the murder told him that the family was trying to keep the details out of the spotlight for whatever reason.

Police were crawling all over it.

It had to be Penny.

Luca figured if he could find the answers to his questions, then it might be one more thing he could use to lead him back to her. To find her.

"One I think is willing to talk about the Smithenson family and the murder," Luca added after a moment.

That had Naz raising a brow. "Oh?"

"Yeah. Or at least, the contact I spoke to said he seemed open and willing to do it. Guess the guy was on to something. He apparently had a story ready to print and everything before it ended up pulled for whatever reason."

Luca would really like to know that reason.

"The Smithenson family probably didn't like what he wrote. It's not like it would be the first time a political family had an arm of control in the media. Shit, that's half the fucking job there, right?"

"What are you two talking about?"

The question from Luca's sister who sat on the otherside of Naz at the table had the two men growing quiet. His friend had been clear—Roz couldn't know *anything*. Not about Luca's job, the things he had found, or the shit he might find in the future. Not until they could get her solid answers and a connection to Penny.

She felt bad enough.

Why add to it?

"Nothing, babe," Naz said, leaning into his wife to kiss her on the top of her head.

It was that moment that one of Luca's favorite people decided to make his little presence known at the table. His godson, Cross, named after his grandfather with the attitude to match his namesake. The five-year-old picked up a slice of French toast from his plate where he sat next to his mother, Luca's sister, and whistled so loud that he shocked the server pouring him a glass of orange juice. His laughter as the juice stained the white tablecloth said the kid had done exactly what he meant to do, especially when he smirked at his father.

"Whoops," little Cross said.

"*Cross,*" Naz said, his sharp tone melting away the boy's smirk.

"Sorry, Papa."

"My fault," the server was quick to say, dabbing at the tablecloth with the white towel she had previously slung over her shoulder.

"No, it wasn't. Someone was just being a pest," Naz muttered.

"Apologize to *her,*" Roz told her son.

The kid sighed.

Always dramatic.

"Sorry," the boy told the server.

Not very sincerely, however.

Win some, lose some.

Luca kind of loved it—little Cross was a bit of a shit when he wanted to be, but the kid got it honestly whether anybody wanted to admit it or not. He was just like his father and grandfather. They had their quirks, and he had his.

The whistling at a pitch loud enough to burst eardrums was his newest thing to do. He liked learning things and once he had mastered the action—like whistling—he did it every chance he could. Luca also taught him how to do it. Naz didn't let him forget it, either.

"Seriously," Naz said at Luca's side. "Thanks, *again,* for teaching him that shit, man."

"Language," came the warning of the boss's wife where she sat beside the man at the head of the table. "There are children here, guys."

"Right," Naz told his mother. "Like I didn't grow up hearing Dad call every other person a motherfucker just because he could."

Light chuckles filtered down at the table. At the very end where Cross sat watching the scene with mild amusement tugging at the corner of his lips, the man only shrugged when he said, "He's not wrong."

"Cross!"

Little Cross whistled again, silencing the rest of his family. This time, it was because a pretty—*younger*—server walked into the room, and the kid's eyes followed her every step. He might have been only five, but the kid already had a preference. Usually blonde.

Luca was to be blamed for that, too.

Hey.

They wanted him as a godfather. Could he really be blamed for passing things on to the kid when they spent time together? Besides, this shit was funny. He had to get his amusement from somewhere.

"*Cross!*" came the collective shouts from his parents.

And grandparents.

That was Luca's cue. He was quick to stand from the table, snapping his fingers at his godson and pointing at the doorway. "Let's go get that orange juice out of your pants, buddy."

The kid glanced down but pushed out of his chair to stand when Luca came up behind him anyway. "My pants are dr—"

"*Bathroom*, kid. Now."

"*Fine.*"

Luca followed little Cross to the doorway, hearing the quiet *thanks* from Naz at the table. He only waved a hand over his shoulder in reply. His silent reply of, *not a problem, man.* Sometimes, his games with his godson got out of hand. He knew how to correct it.

"You know better than that, shithead," Luca told the kid who walked a few feet ahead of him in kid's Doc Martens and a leather jacket that reminded him of his own. "And she was too old for you, anyway."

Little Cross turned to say something to Luca but when his gaze flicked behind Luca, he raised a brow instead. "Hey, Grandpapa."

"Kiddo. Head to the bathroom, yeah?"

The voice of his godfather—the older Cross in the family— had Luca tensing a bit. There was really only one reason the boss would follow him and his godson to the bathroom, and he doubted it was to pat the two of them on the back for the kid's antics.

Luca nodded toward the back hallway. "Go. I'll catch up."

Once little Cross had disappeared into the hallway, Luca turned to face the boss, an apology already on the tip of his tongue. Like his father would always say, it was the respect of the matter. "Sorry, I didn't teach him that to make a scene every chance he could."

Cross rubbed a hand over his mouth, but it did little to hide the smirk forming on his mouth when he replied, "And yet, he does."

"He's just a kid."

In his three-piece suit, the boss looked perfectly fit for his position with his dark stare leveled on Luca. Calm, unbothered, and *cold.* Luca knew that wasn't really who Cross was under the demeanor he put forth, but he held onto it nonetheless. Anything else was bad for business.

"And he's not what I wanted to chat with you about," Cross said. "He's Naz's kid—his problem. Besides, it's not like he's giving his father any less shit than Naz gave me as a kid, right? Fair is fair, and I do like to be fair."

Luca raised a brow, only hearing one thing that interested him. "What do you want to talk to me about, then?"

"Business. Or the business you were discussing with Naz at the table."

Shit.

Nothing got past the boss.

"I was just updating him on something he has me—"

"Ah, he has you on a job, then. You're still ... finding the unfindable, yeah?"

Luca folded his arms over his chest. "It's what I do best."

Cross tipped his chin down, a half nod. "Hmm. You don't want to tell me *what?*"

"Do I need to?"

"No, of course not. You should be careful, though. Especially when looking for things that don't want to be found, Luca. You might not like everything you uncover."

What in the hell did that mean?

Cross didn't give him the chance to ask before the man pointed at the hallway, saying, "Go get my grandson, give him an appropriate discussion about behavior while dining, and *don't* discuss business at the table again. Understood?"

Luca swallowed hard, forgetting that he was a thirty-year-old man who didn't work for Cross Donati's crime family. He didn't have to be. A boss was a boss ... anyone with two brain cells knew it, too.

"Understood," Luca murmured.

• • •

The only hitch in Luca's plan to meet with the reporter he believed had information on the Smithenson family and murder was the fact that the man didn't know they had a meeting at all. Luca wasn't really the whole set-a-date-and-time type. He much preferred to just show up and get shit done because taking people off guard usually ended better for him.

In different ways.

His contact that first brought the reporter to his attention was the same person that ended up giving Luca the information of where to find him, too. The shitty bar in Hell's Kitchen wasn't much to look at and wasn't one Luca had visited before because when he needed to drink himself into oblivion, a place like this wasn't where he liked to do it.

But it didn't matter what he liked.

William Doley liked the place just fine by the looks of the half-empty glass of whiskey sitting in front of him at the bar beside an almost drained bottle of Jack Daniels. The pill bottle two inches to the left of the man's glass was a little concerning once Luca was close enough to read the name of the anti-anxiety meds.

Would the guy even be sober enough to talk?

Luca was about to find out.

Sliding onto a barstool beside the man—he had set himself all the way at the end of the bar in a shadow far away from anyone else—Luca waved at the bartender. "A beer—draft is fine."

He really didn't intend to drink. Driving, and all. The speed of his Ducati never mixed well with even the tiniest amount of liquor, and he wouldn't put his mother through the hell of burying her adult son because he was foolish.

"Sit somewhere else," the guy to his left muttered.

Luca eyed the reporter, his wrinkled shirt and stained, striped red tie. The stain had a yellow tinge, and the first thing that came out of his mouth was, "Did you puke on yourself? That looks like bile."

William didn't even glance down. "At some point. Go away."

"No can do. Why did you delete your social media posts? Apparently, you were going to publish a story about the Smithenson murder last week but then your posts went away ... and no story came out."

That had the drunk—and probably high, depending on how many of those pills he had taken from his med bottle—man glancing up. His head bobbed and swayed as he eyed Luca on the stool next to his. The hazy gleam in his gaze said there were probably *two* of Luca in the man's vision. Maybe this wasn't the best time for a conversation, all things considered, but what choice did he have in the matter?

He needed answers.

This man could possibly give them to him. Given the murder of Elijah Smithenson was the first thing Luca had been able to definitively tie back to Penny in a *real* way that wasn't some bread crumb he found online in the dark web ... well, he wasn't about to back down. Even if that meant having a conversation with a drunk.

"Who the fuck are *you?*" William asked.

Why was that always someone's first question?

Luca shook his head, watching the bartender, and keeping quiet until the man had dropped his glass of beer off and headed back down the bar to tend to someone else. "Don't ask about me. I'm not important here. Not to you or what I want to know, anyway."

William sniffed, reaching for the pill bottle, his hand trembling so much that the pills rattled as he pulled them closer to his chest like it would give him some sense of comfort. That wasn't a good sign. He also didn't answer Luca's question.

So, Luca talked instead.

"It's interesting how much effort the media is going through to *not* talk about the fact it was a murder. Instead, Elijah is being painted as a hero for his family—a bright political career cut short since everyone knew he was going to follow in his father's footsteps. Charitable. Honorable. *Kind.* Most stories this week have barely even mentioned the fact he was murdered. Except you, right? You were going to—"

"Boss made me pull down the posts."

"Are they hiding something?" Luca asked. "The Smithenson family, I mean. I ask about them because if the police knew why he was murdered by now, I'm almost certain I would have been able to pull that information with a few hundred bucks in the right hand. I've got nothing."

"And you won't," William slurred, reaching for his glass after he burped a putrid smell. He downed what remained of his whiskey before his hand went for the bottle to pour some more. "You won't find anything because that's the point. They don't want you to."

"They don't know about *me*."

"Anyone." William waved a wild, trembling hand over his head. "The whole, wide world. Can't stain the image—might cost a donor or two."

"So, they are controlling the media."

"Who *are* you?" the drunk reporter asked again. "Why do you care?"

Luca considered how he wanted to answer that, and if doing so might help his case here. He just needed … *something*. Anything that could lead to another hole for him to dig into where Penny was concerned. A lot of the time, they were pointless rabbit holes. Considering how close he had come to her at the hotel, he wasn't sure this would be the same.

"I'm just a guy looking for a girl," Luca muttered under his breath.

William blinked, smacking his lips as he replied, "Yeah, I bet. Listen, I got nothing to say. Couldn't confirm anything on Elijah … just anonymous sources with information that got me in a lot of shit. The Smithensons, they're everywhere. They watch everything. You start finding their secrets, and they start coming for you."

He surveyed the man at his left again, the liquor and pills … all of it.

"They came after you?"

William laughed dryly. "Can't stain the image."

And what exactly would do that?

The reporter proceeded to pop open the top of the pill bottle before dropping three little pills into his palm. He tossed them back before Luca could attempt to stop him and then reached for the glass he had just poured to wash them down. He wouldn't get more from the man.

That much was clear.

Not having touched his beer, Luca stood from the stool and gestured at the bartender again to gain the man's attention. He slapped down a five-dollar bill, knowing the drink couldn't possibly be worth more than that in a place like this. He pointed at William, tipping his head in the guy's direction as he said to the bartender, "Call an ambulance before he kills himself, huh? There's a reason he's drinking alone in the dark."

He just didn't care about those reasons. Why should he? He had secrets to search for now.

8.

Penny

THE only good thing Penny truly liked about the hotel on the Vegas strip where The League kept her a room, was the view. Add on the small balcony where she could sit and chain smoke while she became lost in her thoughts, and the Bellagio suite basically had it all.

Oh, there was a bed, bathroom, and whatever else she needed was just a phone call to the concierge away. The three-room suite had all the comforts and amenities that a furnished apartment might, too. The decor was modern, expensive, and gave a sense of good taste. Even the artwork on the walls was nice to look at, she supposed.

And she cared nothing for all of that. At all.

Penny wanted a place to sleep, clean, and eat. The only bonus she cared about was the balcony with the view. She had never been the type that enjoyed being closed into any particular space, after all. And despite calling the hotel a home of sorts for the past couple of years once she had earned her right to live outside of The League's complex whenever she was back in the country, well … the hotel suite was as good as anything.

A brown-filtered Marlboro burned between Penny's fingertips, but she wasn't losing herself in memories for the moment. Instead, the laptop on her bare legs kept her pale skin warm despite the bit of wind whipping around the loose strands of her white hair that had fallen from the braid she made earlier. With her free hand, her fingertips danced over the keys, pulling up the dark web browser after turning on the security measures installed by the computer geeks at the complex that could make anything happen with a piece of electronic.

People didn't realize how easy it was to hack something. All someone needed was a Wi-Fi connection—public, especially, but private wasn't safe, either—and they had their easy way in. The rest was child's play to a hacker.

Unless …

Well, it didn't matter.

Penny's devices couldn't *be* hacked now. Part of the job and she was always careful to keep her Bluetooth turned off and *never* connected to any Wi-Fi that wasn't her own. She also rarely took a device out in public where someone else might see.

Was it all a little much?

Maybe.

It was also the advice given to Penny after she joined The League, and she followed it because she needed to. She didn't have a choice when the dark web had been a part of her life since before she could even remember. Now at least, she was the one capable of searching forums and chats and classifieds for whatever she was looking for. She didn't need to bring someone else into it unless the situation called for it.

Sometimes, that was because someone in her business had left a message in the classifieds about seeing her—usually, that was done as a warning to The League or other assassins. Rogues, mostly. Those were more common than not, but their little notes, when not caught, were a possible problem when Penny couldn't afford to leave even the slightest breadcrumb about her existence behind.

If she found something in the usual places of the dark web, then she could get ahead of a situation. Typically, she found *nothing*. Mostly because the people kept employed by her handlers to watch over this sort of thing were half decent at their job.

They did miss shit.

Occasionally.

Which was why Penny also liked to check. Certainly not because she spent hours searching the classifieds with all the right buzzwords.

TU\11. F. Papers. Compliant.

Touched. Unclean. Eleven years old. Female. The girl comes with papers to look legit. *Compliant.* Once someone knew the language, those confusing black and white characters on the screen suddenly became a hell of a lot more horrifying spelled out. Penny *really* shouldn't be putting herself through the punishment of the personal classifieds, but it was a good check and balance for her. The reason why she was here, or part of it.

Placing the cigarette between her lips for a drag, she pulled hard to fill her lungs with smoke. Holding it just far enough from her face to eye the red lipstick stain that matched the color she had painted on her almond-shaped fingernails. Against the ghostly tone of her skin—so pale one could see the blue veins running beneath the surface—the color was quite a contrast.

She liked that.

The white of innocence—which she was *not*. Red like blood; something she knew all too well.

Flicking the ash from the cigarette, Penny went back to the dark web classifieds. She punished herself a little longer, finding more and more reminders to answer all the whys of her current situation, and the reasons for all that she did.

It was only once she had satisfied her masochistic nature that she switched to a common—*popular*—forum for known rogue assassins in the underground criminal world. People who took bounties or worked unmanaged by a larger organization that often took jobs from what they found online in the same places Penny was currently scouring.

Then, something caught her eye.

The white ghost is back—got word she had a job in New York a couple of weeks ago. Did anybody hear anything about it?

That message in the forum had been posted by MG546. It almost made Penny smirk at how everyone knew to stay far away from her when she was in town on a job. To not get in her way. That's what she wanted.

The one and only reply to the original post, only a few seconds earlier before Penny logged onto the forum, came from a username Penny recognized as a guy that watched the forums for any useable—*sellable*—info he could find. The League's hackers who scrubbed the net of her presence on a regular basis, even if it was just the mention of a *white ghost*, said they were pretty sure he was one of the people who fed information to Luca on occasion.

The reply was short and sweet: *The white ghost is already gone—typical job. The hotel in Manhattan. No problems.*

Penny blinked, surprised at how brazen the asshole was in the information he gave about her work in New York. Placing the laptop to the table next to her chair, she grabbed the cell phone she had shoved in the pocket of her cut-off jean shorts and dialed a familiar number.

The League's number one hacker picked up.

"Did you see the latest on the forum?" Penny asked before the girl could even greet her.

"I did not," Jewel replied, "but you know the program we have constantly running will flag it and scrub it. Like it always does."

"Recently posted. Probably too early for the program to catch it. I did. They called me out by the moniker."

"Mmm, the white ghost. You would think they might get a little more … *original.*"

Penny rolled her eyes. "That's not the point. Wipe it, would you? Don't let it stay up until the program finds and flags it. That could take until the morning. I found it; it's there. Scrub it clean."

Jewel sighed heavily, the noise cracking on the phone. "Should I just expect you to call me every time you go on one of your dark web binges? This is the third time this week, Penny. I liked it better when they had you overseas, and the time zones fucked up your ability to contact me on a regular basis. Cree told me to stop enabling you, by the way. I think he's right."

Well, this was nice and all, but …

"Are you going to scrub it or not?"

Jewel muttered something unintelligible under her breath before the clack of computer keys echoed in the background. "Already working on it …" A few seconds later, the hacker said, "Ah, your buddy's little friend again, I see. You know, I looked him up."

"Looked who—"

"Luca Puzza—the one who chases you all the damn time. Figured if he could look for you, then we could look for him. Better to know your common enemy, as the saying goes."

Penny's brow dipped. "And?"

"As someone keeping your existence on the down-low ... he's an ornery fucker that I doubt is going to give it up any time soon. *But.*"

"But what?"

"As a woman with two eyes, a vagina, and working ovaries that make me do stupid things when I see a good looking man, I mean, listen ... it might not be such a bad thing to let the guy catch you. Even once."

Penny didn't even reply to that.

She couldn't because her throat had suddenly grown tight. Like her stomach, too, and the way she squeezed her thighs together at the very *idea.* And this was exactly why she didn't want to respond to Jewel's comment about Luca. That stupid little crush of hers from back when she was a teenager seemed to follow her straight into adulthood; being a different person with a whole new life did nothing for her hormones, apparently.

She was not that weak. A gorgeous man and a few memories from her younger years shouldn't be enough to make her stupid. Yet, it did. So, Penny wouldn't indulge it at all.

Simple.

"I *am* going to follow Cree's advice and stop enabling you, though," Jewel said. "Nothing good comes from you getting on those classifieds and forums, and you know it. Shit, the last time you found old photos of yourself up for sa—"

"Thanks, Jewel. Later."

Penny hung up the phone and tossed it aside before Jewel could say something that might unintentionally send her spiraling into a dark place. God knew she visited that hell more often than she should.

Besides, Jewel wasn't wrong. Neither was Cree. That didn't mean Penny intended on telling either of them they were right.

She considered doing another scan of the forums or classifieds, but it probably wasn't going to do much for her except leave her in a shitty headspace for the rest of the night. Gathering her things, she left the balcony for something better.

Ten minutes later, she sank beneath the hot water that she used to fill the clawfoot tub in the bathroom. So hot, in fact, that steam curled up around the edges of the tub. Setting her arms along the edge for her fingers to hang over the edge, she listened to the droplets of water fall from her digits to the floor.

Drip.
Drip.
Drip.

Her gaze traveled over the length of her legs under the water, to the swell of her hips and the way her breasts lifted and fell with each of her breaths. It wasn't the ghostly shade of her skin that people saw first if they were unlucky enough to see her without her arms and legs covered, but rather the many scars that covered her limbs and stomach.

Crisscrossed marks.

Some red.

Others a faded white.

Penny hadn't cut in years, but she could still vividly and viscerally remember how it felt and what it did for her.

She had been perfect, once. Her skin unblemished and untouched by a razor or whatever other sharp objects she could use to slice into her flesh. Eventually, cutting had been the one thing that numbed her. Before that, it had been the one thing that *freed* her.

Because she wasn't perfect, then.

Nobody wanted a girl that looked like *her*. The monsters wouldn't pay for the privilege of ruining something so ... *broken.*

Where was the fun in that?

But now, the monsters didn't want her at all, and she was still left with a body full of scars, of imperfections. Funny how the thing that had once been the weapon used against her was now her best weapon against everything—and everyone—else.

To hurt others.

To keep from being hurt.

Penny would have continued to spiral in those hellish thoughts, but the ringing of her phone somewhere outside the bathroom kept her from delving any deeper. The special ringtone told her all she needed to know.

The League was calling.

Work needed to be done.

9.

PENNY was right.

She usually was.

The call had come directly from Dare, and without information as to why, Penny found herself walking the familiar halls of The League's complex again. She suspected her handler called her in for a job, or something related to their plan for the group known only as The Elite.

What else would it be?

Rounding the corner at the end of a long hallway that led to the stairwell where she would head up to Dare's office, Penny was entirely unsurprised to find Cree waiting on the bottom step. Legs stretched out and ankles hooked one over the other, the man almost appeared to be sleeping with the way his eyes were closed.

Penny knew better.

"Since when do you lie in wait?" Penny asked, approaching the steps.

She stopped in front of Cree.

He cracked one eye open. "You called Jewel tonight."

"And? I call her frequently."

"Yes, I'm aware." Cree reached up to grab the tail end of his long braid before flicking it over his shoulder. Pushing up to stand to his full, towering height so that she was forced to stare up at him, he turned with a wave of his hand toward the stairs, saying, "Ladies first."

Penny didn't move. "Did she call to tattle on me and complain that I had her do her job?"

"Actually, she was doing what she was told."

Oh?

"Which is?"

Cree shrugged. "Filling us in. When you call, she calls. We like to know what you're doing *when* you're doing it. Especially when it deals with a situation where you might end up doing more harm than good."

"To already bad people? Or by making sure there's no information about me to find on the—"

"By exacerbating your PTSD, Penny."

She let out a hard breath, meeting Cree's gaze when she replied calmly, "I'm fine. And occasionally doing a scan of the dark web for anything I find interesting or that relates to me, and this job doesn't make my PTSD any worse than it already *is*."

"But it does when you find things about yourself. Your *old* self."

That had her jaw tensing. Her teeth clenched so hard, there was no hiding it or ignoring the pain it caused in her molars. Guessing from the way Cree's gaze darted down before coming back up to her face, he hadn't missed it, either.

"Cree—"

"Jewel mentioned something else, too. Luca Puzza."

Penny tried to remain as still as possible. It was the easiest way for her to appear like nothing was wrong and needed that. She needed to be the unbothered, cold human these people had trained her to be even if it wasn't true.

"So now you're having people report back on *everything* they talk about with me?" Penny scoffed, adding just as fast, "And she brought him up, not me."

"Yes, fishing. Because I asked her to."

"*What?*"

Cree chuckled. "There are only a handful of people you willingly talk to on a regular basis. Jewel is one of those because of the very nature of your relationship with her. Even if it is all business. Dare was trying to put feelers out about your feelings regarding the Puzza man trailing you and getting close. You gave nothing away; he still wanted more. So yes, I had Jewel bring it up to see what you would say to someone who *wasn't* above you on the paygrade, so to speak. Someone you might consider a friend of sorts."

"Jewel isn't a friend."

The Native man nodded. "Right, because you don't have those, do you?" *Ouch.*

Penny didn't show the nerve that touched, either.

"Except for that man—*Luca*," Cree clarified, lifting one silk—covered shoulder. "He was a friend, right? You told me that years ago during your initial training when we would do our sessions. Your very first *real* friend, you said. You had a terrible crush on him, but he was too old for you and never acted inappropriately to even encourage your feelings. Nonetheless, you trusted him. Maybe more than even Nazio and Rosalynn Donati. And that's where I keep coming back to with this little issue of him showing up now. That trust ... his friendship."

She refused to look away from Cree but staring at him also gave the man the upper hand of seemingly looking into her soul where she kept most of her secrets close to her heart. One of those secrets, he had just stripped bare and laid out in front of her, as if she might deny it.

"He's not going to be a problem," Penny whispered. "He's just ... a guy."

She wouldn't admit to the many sleepless nights since she came face to face with Luca. Never mind the cold showers when she woke up from lustful dreams that she desperately wished would stop. None of it made any sense; there wasn't a single reason for her to feel those things. They just *were*. She wouldn't feed into it by even discussing it.

Cree wouldn't call her out on any of that—he wouldn't even ask *those* sorts of details. Which was why he kept focusing on her old friendship with Luca and less on the crush she had once admitted to having on the man. Her sexual activities had never been something that Cree put on the table unless Penny did first, and that was only because of her own confusion and fear as she learned to deal with becoming a woman with her own desires and needs after being nothing more than a body with holes to fill for the right price.

For years.

Besides, Penny no longer gave *anyone* that right. She refused to hand over any power to that aspect of her life. Even if that power was only knowledge because, for her, it wasn't an *only* kind of thing. It was too much.

Too much power.

Sex wasn't a weapon. At least, not one she let anyone use against her. Not in any way. Not anymore.

"For what it's worth," Cree said when Penny began to climb the stairs without waiting for him to dismiss her, "I think you're right, and Dare is being his typical, worrisome self because he has to be. He *has* to put the safety of The League above all other things, even his own rationale. A hazard of the job, one could say."

Stopping just long enough to peer over her shoulder, Penny asked, "Then why bother with any of this at all? It seems like a waste of time, and if there's anything we all know about you … you hate that shit, Cree."

"This life isn't forever, Penny. This *place*—what you do now. No one has ever told you that before, but there will be an *after*."

"What does that even mean?"

"After this. The League. Who you are right now. What you're doing. There will be an after. Have you ever thought about what you might want, then?"

Penny hadn't ever thought about what would come after. Maybe because she didn't know there would be one, as that was never discussed when she became a member here. That wasn't the deal but then again … she also hadn't understood the sacrifice she became for this place to do what they did to her, either.

"There's going to be an after?" she asked.

Cree cleared his throat, climbing the stairs until he came to stand beside her. While she usually didn't leave her hotel without a full get-up that would cover her legs, arms, and any other patch of skin where her scars could be seen, she hadn't done that tonight. Instead, she settled on fishnet tights under cut-off jean shorts, and a black tank top.

Her scars didn't bother her. Not anymore. While cutting had eventually become something destructive that she couldn't control, at one time it had been her only savior in a hellish life. It was everyone else that had to look away from her imperfections.

But not Cree.

Reaching over to place his hand on her elbow, his thumb swept the patch of skin where she had once cut so deep that she nearly ruined the muscle there from infection.

"Do you remember what I told you the first time I let you inside the knife room here? You were scared ... a little mouse walking straight into the cat's mouth. You thought even *having* access to those weapons would be too much for your self-control. And I said what?"

Penny's heart thumped hard. "That I would never cut again."

"And you haven't. What else?"

"*I* was the weapon. I just had to learn how to hurt instead of being hurt."

Cree nodded and released his grip on her arm, replying, "But even weapons become dull and unusable, Penny, for one reason or another. We replace them—if we're attached to the weapon, then maybe we display it or use it for something else. This—you—isn't any different. There is always an after; it's all in what you want to do with it." Then, he added with a nod at the stairwell, "Go on upstairs. Job first. Everything else second."

Right.

For now, that was how it had to be.

It was only while Penny walked the hallway that led to Dare's office when she had another thought. Or maybe an epiphany.

Cree brought up Luca—and everything else regarding the man—because he was trying to find out if she wanted him to be part of what came after. All because of what? After years of chasing her, Luca had finally caught up? She didn't know what to do with that at all.

She also didn't know if Cree was wrong.

That bothered her more.

• • •

The last person she expected to see when she walked through the open door of Dare's office was the man standing with his back facing her on the other side of the dominating glass and metal desk. The laptop in front of him glowed to say he was going over something, but she wasn't close enough to discern what. One of the top hackers for The League, Marcel, was kind of a legend around the compound in a lot of ways.

A notorious loner.

Easily provoked.

Dangerous with a laptop.

Specifically, the laptop in front of him that he never went *anywhere* without it being firmly in his hand like an extension of his own body. Supposedly, there wasn't a system the man couldn't breach. As the stories went, he had found himself under the protection of The League after draining the offshore bank accounts of several major criminal figureheads across many organizations. The bounty on his life had been the highest ever known.

And yet, there he stood.

Still alive and well.

"We have a *plan*," Dare snapped, not even noticing Penny just beyond the doorway as he spoke to the infamous hacker. "One we're seeing out one step at a time, Marcel, but if we continue these little side trips and indulging her with them, then we're missing valuable chances to infiltrate the lives of The Elite when we need to the most and when we can make the most impact on the organization."

"What's happened?"

Marcel's shoulders stiffened at Penny's question. Dare, on the other hand, barely even graced her with his attention.

"I said I wanted to be gone by the time she—"

"Yeah, yeah," her handler muttered with a flick of his hand in the hacker's direction. "We all know you hate having to even speak to something with a beating heart that doesn't sign your paychecks."

"I asked a question," Penny said.

She didn't care about their bullshit. That was something they could handle on their own time when she wasn't in the room.

Dare didn't respond.

Or maybe Marcel spoke up before he could, saying to her without ever turning around, "In the process of doing a secondary dive into the Smithenson laptop, I came across an upcoming transaction between him and a wealthy businessman from Florida who makes frequent trips into New York and surrounding states for work-related things. Actually, I found messages between him and a known skin trafficker who works on the dark web for most transactions. He was apparently working on something more permanent than his usual monthly fixes, but the only proof was the fact he was working with the other man. That man was handling all the details."

That made her hesitate.

Only for a moment.

"Which means you found the details of the upcoming ... whatever, how?" she asked.

Marcel finally turned, leaning his back and hands against Dare's desk while he eyed her with a cold stare. "How else, Penny? I traced back the messages, found where they were coming from, hacked into the accounts, and went from there. Shit you don't understand, so let's not waste time going too deep into it."

Fine.

"What kind of transaction?"

She already knew the answer. There was only one thing they would bring to her attention in this case. She still wanted to hear one of them say it.

"A sale," Dare admitted.

Penny grew cold all over.

"Looks like an eleven-year-old girl. Untraceable, practically," Marcel added. "On her end, anyway. The details of the apparent meeting and final transaction, however—"

Penny held a hand up, quieting the hacker as her mind ran through the details she now had and what it might mean. She kept circling back to the same thing … she couldn't let the transaction happen at all.

"And," Dare said, his tone harsh with his irritation, "the cold hits Marcel put through on the deal suggested we're interested in continuing the transaction on behalf of Elijah as associates of The Elite."

"They're willing to see it through," Marcel added quickly.

Dare shook his head, fists balled against the glass top of his desk. "Penny, it's too dangerous to head back to New York right now where they want the transaction to take place. You were just there. You know how this works; we don't go back to the same place twice in a row when you need to be a ghost that comes and goes."

She heard none of that.

"If I'm not there to make the sale, then who will?" she asked quietly.

Dare didn't reply.

Marcel just kept staring.

"Who was there to help me?"

Behind her, a new but familiar voice joined the conversation to say, "You can't help them all, Penny."

Cree had a point.

"Right," she agreed, nodding, "but I can help this one." Then, she pointed at Marcel, adding, "Make contact again—let them know someone will be there to see the deal through."

"Penny—"

"It's *one* girl, Dare," Penny interjected sharply. "And since you apparently have nothing else better for me to do at the moment, then what's the problem?"

"You know the problem."

Sure, she did.

It was never just one girl. There would always be another. Penny would help that one, too, if the opportunity presented itself. It's just what she did.

10.

Luca

SEVEN-THIRTY in the morning was *way* too early for a knock on Luca's apartment door but especially considering he just rolled his ass out of bed. Not even bothering to do more than yank on a pair of sweats he'd been wearing the evening before while he downed a six-pack and watched the game, he made his way to the front hallway of his apartment.

He also didn't bother to check the peephole, but he should have. Yanking the door open, he came face to face with his father. Standing damn near eye-level to one another, neither man said anything.

Luca wasn't accustomed to his father showing up at his place unannounced. If he was being honest ... Zeke hadn't visited in a couple of years. They typically had dinner at his parents' home, or with the Donatis at their place. Maybe one of the family's many restaurants in the city. Even his best friend and sister's home.

Not here.

"You busy?" Zeke asked.

Luca shifted from foot to foot, scrubbing a hand down his unshaven jaw and feeling the prickly hairs tickle his palm while he tried to wake up. His brain was always slower first thing in the morning when he hadn't even been able to guzzle a cup of black coffee. "Not really *busy* just—"

"Waking up, huh?"

He shrugged. "It's seven-thirty, Dad. What else do people do first thing in the morning?"

That probably wasn't the right question to ask considering his father stood on the other side of the threshold appearing as though he had been awake for hours already. Dressed smartly in one of his usual three-piece suits, hair coifed perfectly, and eyes alert. Nothing suggested Zeke was anything less than ready for the day.

Luca couldn't say the same.

"Usually, they go to work," his father replied.

He tried to let that go over his head; normally, it would fly right past, and he could brush it off like nothing. That time it hit him square in the chest, and he felt all of it.

Putting a hand up in the doorway to act as a barricade so that his father didn't get the impression he was about to allow him entrance to his place, Luca said, "And I'll be heading to work soon, too. I've got a ... thing today." Yeah, that was as good as anything in regards to the meeting he planned to spy on later if he got the signal it was still happening from his contact who had been digging into Smithenson, the murder, and anything else that came up which Luca might find interesting. Something had finally come up. It was happening today. "What do you want?"

Zeke sighed, eyeing his son with a sympathy he hadn't expected. "To talk. Or are you not in the mood?"

"Does it matter what I say?"

"Not particularly."

Yeah.

Luca figured.

He could continue to be an ass, but he was quite aware that would only drag this nonsense on, and nobody had time for that. Especially not him. Not today.

"Come on in," Luca muttered, stepping back from the apartment doorway to let his father enter with a wave to the darkened hallway. He hadn't even turned the lights on yet. "I was just about to make coffee. You want one?"

Zeke stepped past the threshold and then Luca, not once taking in the changes to the place since the last time he visited. That was one of the first clues that told him it was very unlikely his father was there for a friendly visit to catch up. While he followed behind Zeke, he let his mind filter through the thoughts and emotions that he usually pushed down whenever he was in the presence of his dad.

They weren't as close.

Not anymore.

Not like they used to be.

Luca tried not to be bitter about that fact, but it wasn't always easy. He understood that his father came from an entirely different generation than him; that Zeke had been raised by men with different values than his own when it came to carrying on the family business and legacy. What was supposed to be important, he had shunned entirely.

At least, to his father.

"Perc or instant?" his father asked when they entered the kitchen.

Luca passed a look at the coffee maker that was only clean because of the three-day-a-week maid he kept well paid to look after his place but stay the fuck out of his shit while she was here. The percolator had been a gift from his sister when he moved into the place—his love of all things coffee meant he should have one, right?

He never used it.

Didn't have the time to wait.

The stupid thing had a timer and everything to make coffee and have it hot and ready by the time he woke up. That would, of course, take time to learn how to program it, and he had little to no interest in wasting precious hours on that.

"Instant," Luca said, heading for the cupboard where he kept the coffee. "Two sugars, right?"

"A half of a teaspoon, actually."

That had him glancing over his shoulder. Sitting on the stool at the end of the island, Zeke raised his brows and smiled slightly at the unspoken question from his son.

"Sugars were high six months ago at my check-up," Zeke murmured, folding his hands together on the kitchen island. "I needed to cut back."

Something else he hadn't known. He also hadn't asked. The tinge of guilt dancing at the edge of his mind made Luca face the cupboards and focus on making coffee instead of delving into something that he wasn't ready to deal with.

Not yet, anyway.

"Your mother wanted me to make you an offer," Zeke said when Luca pushed a steaming cup of coffee across the island. "If you're interested in hearing it."

"An offer for what?"

"You go back to school, finish your law degree, and we pay—"

"I don't need you to pay for anything. I have money."

Not the trust fund promised by his parents once he turned twenty-six and had a clear direction in his life, but still ... he *did* have money. His current job didn't pay in pity or thanks.

"Not to mention," Luca added when his father frowned, "I don't have time to go back to school. And I'm thirty years old; I don't *want* to go back and finish the degree. I haven't wanted to fuck with that mess since I quit a few years ago."

Zeke hummed under his breath. "Right around the same time you began chasing invisible things, son. When you decided the family business wasn't—"

"Did you come here this morning to have another fight with me about my career? Or the fact I'm not doing what you want me to do? Because we've gone over this, Dad, and if it hasn't been obvious enough leading up to now, I don't care what you think."

"It's not too late, Luca."

"What?"

"You're right, you're thirty. It's not too late to get back into the business. Pledge to *la famiglia*, work hard for the next couple of years, prove your worth and get your button. Make yourself a nice spot next to Nazio as his father begins the process of trading seats with his son. Wasn't that what you wanted? What changed?"

Once upon a time, yes.

But life wasn't a fairy tale.

Growing up, all he wanted more than anything was to be Nazio's right-hand man in everything. Life, business, and anything that came up in between. Shit, the guy even married his sister. One of Luca's first memories was running through the forested path that connected their childhood homes with Naz. They had *always* had one another's backs.

That hadn't changed.

He still picked up any call Naz made. Never hesitated to say yes when his friend needed something. He would be loyal to the Donati name and business until the very end. Nothing had changed in that regard.

Luca was also doing what he was doing now *because* of his love for his friend. Because who else was going to get the answers Naz needed?

"Is that happening?" Luca asked.

"Nazio taking over?"

He only shrugged.

Zeke smiled thinly. "It is. Soon. It's something that takes time which is why—"

"You're trying to get me to sit my ass down beside Naz before someone else can."

His father didn't deny it.

"No one will protect him the way you will," Zeke murmured. "Nobody will be as loyal to him as you are. We know it—*he* knows it. His father knows it, Luca. It's why we raised you two like we did. Two generations of Donatis and Puzzas have worked side by side in Cosa Nostra. You and Naz should have been the third. And what, these things you chase, this job of yours, it's more important than the foundation we built for you two? Is that what you want me to tell Cross when the time comes?"

"This *job* ..." Luca dragged in a sharp breath, holding his anger in check but barely. His father, didn't get it; maybe he never would. "I'm good at what I do. I've had contracts all over the country. I've found people that no one else could. So, it's not what you want me to do but it's also what I need to do right now."

Until he found Penny.

Until he had answers.

Luca wasn't the type to give up. And up until he had what he needed to satisfy Nazio, then he would stay right where he was doing what he needed to do. He would take every job that came up in between because it kept his head above water.

"And I'm doing what I promised Naz I would," Luca added.

Zeke leaned back a bit in the chair, observing his son with more intensity than before. "Are you still looking for ... *her*?"

"His father told him to leave it alone—focus on *famiglia* and the business. Not me."

"Because he can't. You don't work for Cross. You are not his made man."

Exactly.

And he wouldn't.

He answered to no one.

Grabbing his coffee for a drink, Zeke downed half of the steaming mug in one go. Maybe his father believed he wasn't going to get what he wanted because the next words out of Zeke's mouth were simply, "What if I asked, Luca?"

"Asked what?"

"For you to stop. Stop searching. Stop all of this. *Be* who you are meant to be. What happens when you find something you're not supposed to?"

"I don't—"

"Only two things happen, then, son. Either someone makes you answer for what you found … or you're left explaining why it happened when no one needed to know. Whichever way the chips fall, it only ends badly for you."

Luca quieted.

So did his father.

Before he could ask Zeke what he meant by that, the ding of his cell phone in the bedroom had him excusing himself from the kitchen to grab the device. A quick check of the screen gave him the confirmation he needed that the meeting later in the day was still a go. Now, he had to get back to doing his job.

Leads on Penny were coming through.

He couldn't leave it alone.

Except by the time he returned to the kitchen, his father was already gone. The only thing that proved Zeke had even been there in the first place was the empty coffee mug sitting in the sink, and the lingering scent of sandalwood and crisp spice. His father's cologne.

Everything else was exactly the same.

For Luca, nothing had changed.

• • •

The reporter might not have wanted to talk, but he gave Luca a bone to find. Really, that was all a dog needed to start digging.

Or rather, *Luca.*

Once he knew the area to look for—like the dead Smithenson man and any secrets his family was attempting to keep hidden—the only thing left to do was uncover them. Well, he needed the right people looking in the right places to uncover them, so to speak.

In the process of his hacker contact digging through every single morsel of information regarding the political family that he could, the guy managed to stumble upon rumors of an upcoming business deal. One between a dead man and another guy, a businessman from Florida, who was very much alive.

Two things were important in that information to Luca. Dead men didn't make deals—business or otherwise. And there was always a little bit of truth to every rumor. It took a bit more digging, some money shoved into the right hands to figure out *why* the deal was still apparently on the table despite Elijah being dead, and Luca had what he needed.

A meeting at a pizzeria in Hell's Kitchen between associates of the now-dead Elijah Smithenson and the Florida businessman. Someone else decided to see the deal—whatever it was—through.

Luca still had a few issues with the whole thing. The most important being the fact that he was chasing what he figured would end up being nothing more than another rabbit hole. There was no reason to suspect the meeting had anything to do with Penny. She had been long gone from New York for weeks without even a whisper of a possible return either from the underground criminal networks or on the dark web.

Unfortunately, Elijah was still Luca's only lead he could connect back to her. Even dead, it was possible that whatever affiliations he had could somehow provide Luca with the details he needed to fill in some blanks. He would take anything at this point.

Everything else had long gone cold.

Besides, spying on the meeting in Hell's Kitchen would take all of an hour out of his day. Maybe even less, depending on how it went. Then, he could head over to meet with a man in lower Manhattan whose employee had up and disappeared with a hundred grand of the company's cash that he wanted to be returned as soon as possible.

So, without any details as to what the meeting in the Kitchen would entail or the supposed deal taking place, Luca found himself sitting in the passenger seat of his black Bentley watching the view into the pizzeria through large bay windows. He'd visited the business a couple of hours before—just long enough to grab a slice of pizza and place two bugs on both sides of the dining floor. That covered all his bases and would let him listen in when the guests of the hour finally arrived.

At worst, he was wasting his time. At best, he might gain something useful that opened up a new door or answered questions.

Luca wasn't hopeful.

He also wasn't giving up.

The other thing he hadn't done?

Tell Naz.

Partly because his friend was busy this week and when he wasn't, Naz was always with Roz who he didn't want to know they were still looking for Penny. The other reason he hadn't told his friend that he might have another lead to follow was simply because … well, if he wasn't hopeful, then why should he give false hope to Naz?

He wouldn't.

Couldn't.

A black car with darkened windows pulled up across the street at the same time Luca's phone dinged in his lap. He pulled the phone up, unlocking the screen to read the message as he eyed the new arrival at the same time.

Except he couldn't do both.

And one was more interesting.

The woman who stepped out of the backseat, that was. Her pin-straight black hair wasn't covered by a hat this time. His slightly rolled down window allowed him to hear what she said to the man who had opened her door just seconds before.

"They'll be here in five," the man said. "And you know the rules."

"Ten minutes—max," Penny replied. "I know."

Her voice hadn't changed a bit; it was still light like air. Musical, even. But she was nothing like the girl he used to know.

Across the street, Penny and the man headed for the pizzeria. Luca finally checked that message on his phone.

It was his hacker contact.

With more info.

The guy from Florida—finally found what I was looking for. Known trafficker. Kids, mostly. Watch yourself, Luca. That's a slippery slope.

He didn't have time to process what that news meant. A second car had just pulled up to the pizzeria.

Two men in suits stepped out.

No one else.

No … *child.*

He didn't know why, but something told him bad shit was about to happen.

11.

Penny

A great wig, makeup to enhance one's features, and colored contacts could do a great deal to change someone's appearance. It was the only extra precaution Penny could really take for her second trip to New York within weeks. It also wasn't nearly enough to satisfy the worries that Dare—and Cree, occasionally—continued to voice right up until the moment she stepped on the private jet.

Nonetheless, while she watched her reflection in the glass of the pizzeria's bay window, she figured she hadn't done a half-bad job on making herself look different than the last time she was in the city. Her skin wasn't as ghostly with a pink-toned foundation, a touch of bronzer, and a dark contour to make her face appear more oval, and her jawline a bit softer. Add in the black kohl she had smoked around her eyes with a winged flair and black wig, and she was one step up from her usual ghostly paleness.

Not by much, though.

She also hated heavy makeup. And wigs. Contacts, too, the itchy bastards. Since landing in New York only hours earlier, she learned something else that she didn't like very much, as well. This entire city—maybe the state.

She felt too comfortable here.

Or ... *comforted.*

A sense of nostalgia came along to fill her whenever she recognized a building that she had once visited. Or worse, a memory hit her while she drove down a familiar street and then she was lost to a different time and place that shouldn't matter to her anymore because she wasn't the same person she used to be.

Frankly, Penny blamed Cree.

And his mention of the *after.*

Or what could be.

It had been on her mind for days. The sleepless nights that followed certainly didn't give her anything else to think about, either. All fun things.

It was only the squeak of the chair next to hers that finally pulled Penny from her thoughts. They had barely been sitting down inside the business for more than thirty seconds, but she was already distracted *and* annoyed. Neither of those spelled good things for her. Or for the man next to her.

She couldn't afford to be anything but ready at the moment. This deal— even if it was just a sham for her to help a trafficked girl—would be over before it even began if the men she was supposed to meet to make the transaction thought something was up. Even if that *something* was just her distraction.

"Stop fidgeting," Penny told her companion.

Chase was his name. Another assassin for The League who just so happened to be available to take this trip with Penny and see the job through. Cree tried to play it off like it was nothing more than coincidence, but she didn't think so. Chase was one of the few people she could stand to talk to for more than a few minutes at a time—he'd also been on the team that trained her … and the first man she ever allowed to sleep with her.

Not in the sex sense.

Although, he *had* offered.

No, on one of her few free nights out during that first year of her training, Penny did a stupid thing that left her less than sober and in need of a chaperone to make sure she didn't choke on her vomit in her sleep. Chase was there … he did the right thing.

Earned her trust, anyway.

A rare feat.

So few people had it.

"Not fidgeting," Chase replied. "Getting a better look."

"At what?"

"Our oncoming company. Check it out."

Well, they were timely.

Penny would give the sex traffickers that, but not much else. They weren't worth anything more, honestly. And if this were any other job for Penny, then those two men stepping out of the driver and passenger seats of a nondescript black vehicle wouldn't make it out of the pizzeria with a heart still beating in their chest.

But today wasn't about death.

It was something else entirely.

A victim was on the line.

"Where's the girl?" Penny asked, never taking her stare away from the men shutting their doors and doing a quick sweep of the street and movement around them. "She should be—"

"Maybe in the back. You know how this works out in broad daylight. Money first, transaction later. Sometimes at a different location. Play their game, and we see how it goes."

Chase made sense.

Penny still didn't feel right.

"That wasn't the agreement made when contact was made," Penny murmured.

"Shit changes all the time," Chase replied. "You know that."

That didn't mean she trusted anyone but especially not skin traffickers who specialized in the trade of *children*. If there was anything she learned in her life, it was that monsters would always do the most monstrous things when given the chance.

Her current problem was bigger.

She didn't have the time to reconsider their situation or the meeting. The men entered the pizzeria before Penny and Chase could discuss a change in *their* plans, forcing them to go ahead with their original one.

The thing was, that required a *girl*. One that was supposed to be delivered in exchange for the hundred grand that was to be transferred into an offshore bank account during the meeting. But there was no girl ... and she was pretty sure there wasn't one waiting in the back of the black car—that they had left running—outside.

The few patrons of the pizzeria barely looked up from their pizzas or phones when the men entered. All the details had already been passed between the two parties. Chase and Penny could arrive first—although real names hadn't been given, of course—and would sit on the right side of the bay windows together. Easily seen. Quick to leave when it was over. She would wear a black, long-sleeve dress with a red necklace. Chase would also wear a black suit with a red tie to match.

There was no mistaking them.

The men had no issue spotting them.

"Get this done," Chase said, standing from the table as the men approached without greeting, "and we get the fuck out, right?"

"Right," Penny agreed at the same, quiet level. "Once we have the girl."

"Not if it means—"

"Where's the product?" Penny asked the taller of the two men, the one on the left with a scar that ran down his cheek and left the side of his face droopy when they came to a stop only two feet away from their table. "Money won't be transferred without at least an inspection."

"Sorry, my wife is a bit ... particular about this sort of business," Chase added, smiling tightly. "But she is correct. We were promised a look at the—"

"There is no girl," Scarface said.

Shorty on the right quickly added, "The Elite send their regards to the white ghost."

They *wouldn't*. They wouldn't be so brazen; so *stupid*. There wasn't a chance.

And yet, Penny knew in that moment how badly of a mistake they had all made. *Her*, actually. Just her. She had made a terrible mistake. Maybe it was the emotion involved in these things that made it all unclear for her.

It didn't matter.

Dare had been right—The Elite finally figured out what was happening to each of their members and that every kill Penny had made up, including her last, was all connected to them, their organization, and their business of trafficking children for wealthy pedophiles.

It was too late to fix her mistake.

Her *ignorance* ...

In a split second, as both men reached for the guns hidden in holsters beneath their jackets, Penny was all too aware that she was in the final moments of her life. The men paid no mind to the people or the employees of the business. They were clearly there with a mission—a job to get done.

Chase hit her from the side when the first gunshots rang out. Glass shattered—likely the window behind them. The screams echoed.

Penny was already reacting even as her body crashed to the floor with Chase's heavy body falling on top of hers. She grabbed the gun that she kept in the holster at her inner thigh and the one Chase kept at his side before he could reach for it himself.

With a gun in each hand, she aimed around the table and fired two shots. They both hit the man with the scar, straight in the face, marring him further and taking him to the ground.

"*Move,*" she snapped at Chase.

The only sound he made was a grunt when a bullet plugged into his back. She quickly realized it wasn't the only gunshot he had taken. The one that ended up in his chest was bleeding through his button-down over Penny's black dress.

He wasn't dead.

Yet.

He would be.

Soon.

"*Masters?* Masters, look at me!"

Penny slipped out from under Chase on trembling legs as her adrenaline kicked into high gear. The only asshole left alive, while the few patrons scattered to the exit, was currently leaning over his partner in crime. As she stood to her full height, the guy finally realized she was still alive. His gun started to raise as she lifted her own.

Bang.

The bullet plugged between his eyes. He hit the ground, slumped over his partner's corpse, but it wasn't over.

Not even close.

All it took was Penny glancing to the side where the window had been shattered by an earlier bullet. She could have tried to help Chase. If it weren't for the two men who rushed out of the backseat of the still-running vehicle outside. Like the men dead on the pizzeria's floor, they also wore black suits. And had guns in hand.

She had hoped a girl waited there for her to save from a far worse fate—the same hellish existence she had been forced to live through for years. She couldn't have been more wrong. Now, Chase was dying on the floor because of it, and her one option was to leave him there.

Penny headed for the back of the restaurant. Her companion would die alone; she would hear his final grunt for the rest of her life knowing it had been her fault, like so many other things.

What choice did she have?

It was her only chance to get out of this alive.

12.

Luca

LUCA had realized early on that bad shit was about to go down in the pizzeria. Long before he heard the sale of a girl-child mentioned between Penny and her associate. Before the bullets were shared between adversaries, he'd known. He couldn't say *why*, exactly, but that heaviness in the pit of his stomach only grew in weight the longer he sat in his vehicle and waited for whatever it was to happen.

And then it did.

Fast.

Horribly.

Spectacularly.

Violence tended to be that way. Without warning and uncompromising. No prejudice and available to anyone at an unfortunate distance. He heard the shots second—the screams next. The first thing had been an unfamiliar voice crackling over the comm in his ear as he listened to the conversation happening inside the pizzeria.

A long time ago, Luca learned there were two kinds of people in the world. Those who ran away from danger, and the ones who ran *into* it. The people who sought danger had different reasons for doing so while the ones who ran from it only had one—to save their lives.

Luca didn't like dangerous situations. He did have a sense of self-preservation despite what his profession and family legacy might suggest. And yet, often, he still found himself running into the danger instead of away.

Because he didn't have a choice.

Especially this time.

The two men who stepped out the backseat of the black car that pulled up mere minutes after Penny and her associate had arrived didn't notice Luca exiting his own vehicle. The men roughly shoved past the people flooding out of the pizzeria while he headed for the alleyway on the side of the business.

Chances were if Penny had made it out of the gunfight alive inside—and by the crackling voices in his comm, she *had*—then she wouldn't take on another set of gunmen just for the hell of it. Even those who ran into the danger knew when to back down.

It was common sense.

68

So, Luca used some of his own, too. She might not want his help in this situation, but he also wasn't going to give her a choice in the matter.

His mind bounced from one thing to another, desperately trying to catch up to speed with all the things he had learned in the span of mere minutes. This wasn't at all how he thought the day would go down; he was only supposed to spy on a meeting, not *this*. Part of him thought it was just luck on his part but another believed someone—or something—had put him here today because he needed to be.

He could deal with it later.

Maybe.

Was the meeting a set up to draw Penny out? It sure seemed like it based on the things he heard and what followed. That assumption of his was only compounded when he rounded the corner at the end of the alley to find another man in a black suit. With his back turned to Luca and his finger pressing at the comm in his ear, it was clear the guy was backup.

Waiting.

For Penny, likely.

Just in case she came out the back—or her friend, even. He probably parked somewhere nearby and walked to his position, so he wouldn't be seen.

Luca didn't even think about his next actions. Drawing the gun he kept holstered at his back, the man didn't even see the shot coming. The bullet plugged into the back of his head. At the same time his body hit the ground, the backdoor of the pizzeria flew open and slammed into the brick from the force alone.

She almost stumbled in her heels; damn near fell over the body when she took two long strides beyond the doorway. Her black wig was a tangled mess, and the red smears on her chest continued down the front of her dress.

Blood.

He didn't have time to react; neither did she. Her icy gaze darted from the man on the ground to the gun Luca still had raised. He hadn't even had time to lower it.

"*Luca*," he heard her breathe.

Was that anger?

Shock?

Something else?

The shouts coming from within the pizzeria and the way Penny glanced back at the door just before it closed reminded him that he didn't have the opportunity to think it over right then. They had to *move*.

And fast.

"This way," he said to Penny, nodding straight. "Follow me."

He was already passing her and the dead body by, but she didn't move and inch.

"Why?" she asked.

"Because I assume you want to live," Luca replied, his stare locking onto her gaze, surprised to find brown eyes staring back at him instead of her usual bright blue. Contacts. It made the five feet that separated them seem a lot smaller in those moments. Her eyes were still the same; wide and bright despite the sadness that was ever-present. The demons that haunted her always showed there no matter how hard she tried to hide them. "And I know these alleyways better than *anyone*. Grew up on them, you know? I can help. Let me."

Her unease at the very sight of him was obvious. No doubt, she wanted answers for why he was there or his motives. He understood but now wasn't the time. She looked like she was going to argue, but only for a second.

"We don't have time for questions, Penny."

Penny nodded once. "Let's go."

Yeah.

Before the assholes burst out of the door as she had.

They barely made it around the corner at the other side of the back alley into a new one before the bang of the metal door hitting brick echoed again. Penny had quite the talent for running in a pair of four-inch stiletto heels, keeping up with Luca's pace every step of the way as he navigated the maze of alleys in the familiar area. Not that he had time to appreciate it.

Every time he thought they were far enough to take a break, he was proven wrong. Their pursuers were never too far behind. It wasn't like the men were quiet about their chase, shouting orders back and forth while he kept moving forward with Penny right on his heels.

"Where are we going?" Penny asked when they rounded another corner.

"Not far now. Ditch the wig."

"*What?*"

Luca ripped off his leather jacket and handed it over, barking, "Put this on and ditch the wig—*now.*"

She did as they came to a dank alley with only one door and several trash dumpsters. Moving in front of the dark green metal door that had clearly seen better days with all its dings and scuffs, Luca banged his fist five times against the middle. There wasn't a handle on the outside but that was common for this place. There was only one official entrance but even that was hard to find.

Which was the point.

He banged on the door again.

To no avail.

Yet.

"This is a dead end," Penny hissed at him.

"Only on the surface," he replied. "Just trust me. We need a minute. That's all."

"We don't have a minute. They were right behind us!"

"*Quiet.*"

She'd tossed the wig into a dumpster. His jacket fit her well, though. The shouts from outside the alley gave away the fact that the chase wasn't over yet, and if he didn't figure out something soon, then ...

Fuck it.

Luca banged on the door one more time and then he moved for Penny. He didn't give her time to react before he reached down and ripped three holes into her black tights. Exposing her thighs and knees, he rubbed his hands into the dirt on the ground and marred her creamy, white exposed skin to dirty her up.

"What the fuck are you *doing*?" she asked, the pitch of her tone raising to a level he had never heard.

"Shut up and play along."

"Play—"

He flipped up the hood of his sweater, thrust his hands into the messy braid that had fallen from her wig to mess it up even more, and then slammed her back into the brick wall of the building. The instinct of self-preservation kicked in for Penny, making her fist Luca's sweater when her burning gaze met his.

Fight or flight.

He knew that all too well. Too bad he couldn't give her the opportunity to do either.

Luca banged on the door right beside them one more time. "We just need another minute. That's all."

"You're going to get us kill—"

No, he wasn't.

Trust was earned, though.

"Hey, I hear something over here, man!"

Luca didn't have any more time to prepare Penny for what he was going to do next, so he just did it. His lips crashed down on hers without warning. Her hands flexed harder into his sweater, simultaneously pushing him away but then pulling him closer when her eyes blew wide, and she realized what he was doing. The fast exploration of his hands down the curves of her hips came to a stop at the tight cinch of her waist, and he felt every single shiver that he earned from her for it, too.

He liked it.

Didn't want to admit it.

But he *did.*

She tasted like pure heat and felt like silk. Even with the dirt on his palms as a barrier between his hands and her body. Even with her trembling lips working against his. Her shuddering breath let him deepen the kiss, make it look *real*.

Even if it felt that way already.

He didn't have a choice. That's what he would keep telling himself, anyway. They only needed another minute and—

"*Yo*—what the fuck are you two doing?"

One of the dumpsters had allowed Luca and Penny a bit of privacy from the two men standing at the end of the alleyway in the light. The shadows helped even more to keep them from further view.

He bared his teeth and glared. "Fuck off—I paid for this. Get your own."

Luca knew how it would appear. A guy and a hooker in a dank alley next to a dirty dumpster. The dead end wouldn't lead the pursuers to anything worth chasing. And those men weren't really looking for him in the first place.

The two men passed a look between each other. Penny's leg came up to hook around Luca's hip, showing off one of the rips and dirt on her skin. Nothing else, though. It did, however, push their bodies closer together, doing *nothing* to hide the erection growing under his jeans.

Fuck.

Why was his throat so tight?

He swallowed hard. "You fucking mind, or what?"

At least, he hid the heat from his voice. The nerves, too. Barely.

"Sorry, man," the guy on the left said.

"You see a bitch with black—"

"Does it look like I'm looking for other people?" Luca barked.

Both men flipped their hands high, a silent apology. They moved on out of view of the mouth of the alley without another word. The air he released felt like relief but did nothing to ease the pressure in his chest and pants.

He reached over and banged on the door one more time.

Come on, Freddie, he thought. *Come on, man.*

Under his hands that still hadn't taken from Penny's body, he felt all of her tremors. Every single one. And the way it increased when his fingers flexed against her waist, holding her tighter.

He met her gaze again.

Wide, and *unsure*.

"Don't be scared," he told her.

For so many reasons.

Their current situation, the fact he was a man and touching her when he knew …

"I'm not scared," she replied through clenched teeth and a tight jaw.

In all the years Luca had chased after this girl—*no*, a woman now—he had pushed aside the knowledge that once, she had looked at him differently than she did other men. Her young crush on him, that even she admitted was silly, wasn't something he could indulge back then. Or even wanted to when all he could see when he looked at her back then was a broken girl desperately trying to make it one more day. He'd been her friend; nothing more.

He couldn't say the same at that moment. It fucked him straight up.

"I know," Luca murmured.

He could still taste her on his lips, and the tightness of his throat only increased when he tried to swallow the feeling away.

Penny opened her full, pink lips to say something else but *finally,* the door opened at their right. The familiar face of a man Luca had been cursing for the last several minutes peeked out of the doorway. Freddie Jonesburg cocked a brow like *he* was the one being inconvenienced.

"Puzza—what the fuck do you want?"

"A favor," Luca replied.

Freddie eyed the situation happening outside his door. Luca at least had the decency to put some distance between himself and Penny, even though he couldn't help but keep one hand on her waist. "Like what kind of favor?"

"A room. Maybe for a few hours or the night, or—"

"You pay it back whenever I want?"

"Just ask," Luca agreed, "and I'll do it."

Freddie nodded once and pushed the door open wider. "Come on in, then. Last time I saw you was what, last year when you were hiding out from some fuck in Brooklyn that you pissed off, right?"

"First of all, I didn't piss him off. I just took something that he took from someone else. He had it coming."

Or *mostly.*

Luca entered the building first, but Penny soon followed. The dark hallway was dimly lit by a single bare bulb over the stairwell at the far end. Red walls. A metal staircase. It wasn't much to see, but the exits of the underground haven rarely were to begin with. Equipped with everything from rooms to sleep in, and a bar to drink when one wanted, a guy could hide out for as long as he could stand to stay out of sight as long as he was willing to pay the price to stay. Although, with a recognizable face like Luca's because he'd been around doing business here before … he had a bit of pull in some cases.

Freddie was already climbing the stairs not even bothering to wait for the boarders he had decided to room without more than the promise of a returned favor in the future.

"What is this place?" Penny asked.

Luca shrugged. "It's used for a lot of things. None of which we ask about."

Penny followed behind Luca in silence; he was grateful.

All he could think was *what happens now?*

13.

Luca

THE room Freddie said he had available for Luca and his guest—he refused to give Penny's name or even a fake one—wasn't much to look at. A sketchy, queen-size bed with a bare mattress although a quick smell of the folded blankets at the foot said they had at least been washed.

By who, Luca didn't know.

He also wouldn't ask.

The singular dresser with five drawers had seen far better days. Dings and chipped paint weren't a decorative touch he preferred but as he didn't plan to use it anyway, what did it even matter? A small mirror with a crack in the bottom, left-hand corner hung over a steel sink that jutted from the wall covered in peeling, yellowed wallpaper. He wasn't even sure the rusty pipes under the sink would work to bring water to the taps.

Under the soles of his feet, wood floors that had seen better days creaked with every step he took around the small space. The room couldn't be larger than ten feet by ten feet. The tiny window over the lone piece of furniture in the room other than the bed—the dresser—wouldn't even fit a small child through it.

But the place would do.

For now.

"Toilet and shower down the hall," Freddie said from the doorway.

Penny passed Luca a look that he didn't return. Instead, he told the man, "Thanks."

"We've got the cook downstairs from six until six. The bar, too. And the window won't open. Don't bother trying."

"Got it."

"Let me know if you need more than a day. I'll see what I can do. Anything you want me to know?"

That time, Luca did glance Penny's way. She had turned her back to the man in the doorway while she surveyed the small closet with four, lonely wire hangers left on the rack. He didn't think she was interested in the objects, but she *was* avoiding talking as much as possible.

"Yeah," Luca muttered. "If anyone asks, we're not here."

"Who are *we*, exactly?" That time, Freddie pointedly stared at the back of Penny's white-blonde head. "Never knew you to bring guests ... you working, or—"

75

"Something like that."

Luca doubted the answer satisfied the man, but Freddie didn't show it. He also wasn't the type to be messed with which was why the underground haven was a good place to lie low for a while if needed. Wide-shouldered, built like a brick shithouse and about as tall as one, too, the man could go a round or two without even needing a breath.

The people who *could* cause a problem for Freddie tended to leave the man alone because he never took sides in anything. He simply offered what he had to whoever needed it as long as they didn't bring him any issues in the meantime.

A simple give and take. One Luca respected as did many others.

"That all?" he asked Freddie.

The guy sucked air through his teeth, giving Penny one last look before he turned on his heels to leave the room altogether. Grabbing the door handle to shut out the noise from down the hall, he only stopped long enough to say to Luca, "Yeah, but you know the rules."

"Of course. And as long as everyone is told we're not here … they'll be followed. We cool?"

"Sure. Enjoy your evening."

Yeah.

Luca doubted that.

The door to the room wasn't closed longer than ten seconds before Penny turned to face Luca. Her previous disinterested expression had been replaced with a heat he hadn't expected. And not one that would end well.

No, she was … *angry.*

"I've got *nothing,*" she snapped. "No phone. No line of contact to my handlers. I don't know what the fuck this place is, but I'm pretty sure it's not safe to go wander the halls and find a phone. If we kept running, then maybe I could have—"

"What, got away again?" Luca scoffed. "Doubt it, sweetheart. Those alleys just keep getting longer and longer. They were too close. I had to make a choice, and I knew this place was close by. Freddie and his people won't let anybody in here to search for shit. That's now how it works. You're safe until you think, or *know,* it's clear to go."

"And how am I supposed to know when that is if I don't even have a phone—"

Luca closed the distance between them and shoved his hand into the inner pocket of his leather jacket that she was still wearing. Penny jerked slightly away from him, but he was all too aware of the way she watched him—her gaze soft, but wary. Pulling the item out that he was looking for, he held off on handing it to her.

Just long enough to say, "I knew Freddie or one of his guys would hear the knocking. I just needed a couple of minutes. I wouldn't have kissed you or made it look like we were doing any—"

"It's fine."

She said that too fast. He heard that clearly, and the air in her words, too. Also, she wouldn't meet his gaze, determined that everything else in the room was apparently more interesting than him at that moment.

"It's not," Luca said. "If that freaked you out, a guy being on you like that after everything that's been done to you—"

"Could you *not?*"

Luca straightened at the sharpness in her tone and the sting of her gaze when it leveled on him. Unashamed and without fear, she challenged his notions of her with nothing more than her presence and a look. He had to keep reminding himself that this woman he finally found was not the same one he had been chasing. *Years* had changed her; circumstances and life turned her into someone else.

Not that it was a bad thing.

It just ... *was.*

"I'm not a fragile doll that breaks apart every time someone comes within breathing distance of me, Luca," Penny said, yanking his jacket off and then throwing it to the bed behind him. "And I know how to make someone *stop.* You got me?"

He nodded.

"Good," she muttered.

"Here." He held out the phone that he'd taken from the jacket. One of two phones he kept on hand—but this one was for work, only. "It's a burner. No one's listening in. You're welcome to use it. Call your ... handler, or whatever."

Penny eyed the phone in his outstretched hand like it was diseased. He didn't move a muscle until she did finally take the device. A minute later, he listened from where he sat on the foot of the bed while she spoke to someone she called *Cree.*

"Definitely dead, yeah," Penny said. "Probably before I even made it out the back. Is someone going to retrieve his ... no? Why the hell not?"

A beat passed.

Penny scowled. "Fine—but he's got a kid. *Had* a kid. Someone's going to tell them he's not going to be around, right?" She shifted from foot to foot, watching her reflection in the mirror as the person on the other end of the call replied before she said, "At least two are looking right now. And yeah, I can stay out of sight until the mess is cleaned. How long do you—"

A curse fell from her lips.

"Tell Dare he can fuck off, too. This wasn't something we could have seen coming. Nobody knew the deal was bait to draw me out. *Nothing* suggested that in the contacts our man had with them. Don't let him call anything off, Cree. We're too close and—"

Another minute passed. Penny grew more irritated by the second. Luca couldn't help but notice how she didn't mention him or his involvement in what happened at the pizzeria.

"Fine, I don't move until someone comes looking for me. Got it."

Penny offered nothing else before she hung up the call. Before Luca could even ask for his phone back, she proceeded to beat it against the side of the metal sink until the device crumbled into a hundred broken pieces on the floor.

He just ... stared.

Like an idiot.

"Why the fuck did you do that?" he demanded.

Penny didn't even turn around. "Because I can't trust you not to trace the call back, or *try*. Not that it would do you any good because my handlers can't be found that easily. Either way, I can't be too safe with you."

That pissed him off.

"What, like I didn't help you today? I'm *still* helping you!"

She didn't reply.

That annoyed him more.

Getting to his feet, Luca asked, "How are your people even going to find you? Rumor is you work for an organization called The League, right? I hear they don't take kindly to their members going AWOL."

Penny laughed darkly, turning around and placing her hands on the edge of the metal sink while she faced him. "Nice try. Who do you think I was just talking to, anyway? God? They can find me anywhere in the world within a few feet of my current position. I don't need to be carrying anything for them to do it, either. I *am* what they track."

What?

"Are you saying they have a chip in—"

"How did you find me today?" she interjected, reverting back to the calm, unbothered demeanor like a light switch had been flipped. It was almost disconcerting to him how easily she could mask or change her emotions altogether. That was new, too.

"Luck," he admitted. "I wasn't there looking for you."

"Don't think I'll believe that when less than a few weeks ago, you showed up at *another* job of mine, too. I'm not that stupid, Luca. We *will* find out who you've made contact with that's been feeding you information on me, and it will come to an end. Do you understand that? If you keep causing problems and showing up where you're not supposed to be, the next step is to make sure you can't. *Permanently.* I'm trying to warn you here. Stop whatever this stupid shit is before they—"

"They—The League?"

Penny dead stared him.

Luca didn't care.

"Give me something," he urged, widening his arms like he was asking for peace. "I'm only trying to do what Naz and Roz can't. You know that's why I'm here; why I've *always* looked for you since the day you went missing. I changed my entire life to look for *you*."

Now, he was wondering why.

Penny was unfazed. "I'm asking you to stop."

"I *can't*." Luca chuckled, shaking his head when he muttered, "I could make a call right now—get my sister and Naz down here. All they want is to see you, know you're okay, and *talk*. After everything they did for you, can't you give them that at least?"

"You do that, I'm gone."

Luca's brow raised at the threat. "Seriously?"

"This time, I might not leave you alive."

"Shit, don't promise a good time, Penny."

His comment had zero effect.

That was the thing that sent his anger spiraling more than anything else had in their entire conversation. How she seemed so ... *unaffected*. Indifferent, even. The mere mention of Luca's sister and best friend, people who had cared and loved and protected Penny until she turned eighteen and then disappeared, did absolutely nothing for her.

Or so it seemed.

"They *love* you. Fuck, they thought you loved *them*! You can't be that removed from what happened five years ago that you don't even care about them or what you did to them when you left. *Why?* That's all they want to know, Penny. Just tell me why."

His shouts did nothing, too. The rare sight of his temper when he stepped closer to her wasn't even a blip on her radar. She was like ice. Beautiful, cold, and unmoveable. Who was this woman?

"Don't you care at all?" he asked, his tone tempering a bit. "Your godson is five years old. We still call him little Cross but not to his face because he doesn't like people thinking he's tiny. He still carries around the bear with you made for him, though. Listens to the recording of you playing the piano every—"

"*Shut up.*"

Ah, there it was.

Luca found the nerve. He hit it with a punch that sent Penny pushing away from the sink to close the distance between the two of them until she was face to face with him and her stare was anything but *cold*.

"He knows your name," Luca murmured. "He knows your face; Roz kept pictures. They do love—"

"I'm protecting them!"

His shouts had done nothing. Hers cut into his heart like a hot knife through butter.

"From what—*who*?" Luca demanded. "Do you know where we come from—who *Naz* is? The Donati family isn't little fish, babe. Don't be stupid."

Penny didn't even blink. "From me, people like me ... people I came from and—"

That was it.

She clammed up.

A door had almost opened, but Penny slammed it shut before Luca could even get his foot on the threshold.

"I can't go back," she told him, "and it's better if they don't know ... so neither will you. I won't say more. Because the more you get, the faster you chase me, Luca. Today, it might have been a good thing but the next time, it might kill us both."

Luca's jaw ached from how hard he clenched his teeth. "I'm not going to stop."

"You don't know *anything* about the world I live in. It's not like yours. This is dangerous."

"Not any more or less dangerous than mine."

She barked out a dark laugh, her gaze hardening when she asked, "Do you wanna bet?"

Luca knew her history all too well. Some, he had learned during her time with his sister and friend. A lot, he stumbled upon in his first few years chasing after her. The shit the public hadn't known—how deep the pedophile ring really ran that her father was heavily involved in and used to traffic her sexually up until she was nearly twelve. Adding all of that knowledge to what he had seen and heard today, he had to wonder ...

He couldn't stop himself from asking, "That's what you're doing, isn't it? You're tracking them all down ... you're killing pedophiles."

Penny only smiled.

Wicked.

Icy.

"Oh, it's so much worse than that, Luca. And you're already in over your head—just stop before you drown."

14.

Penny

PENNY figured she would be able to do a few hours locked in a room with Luca. Maybe a night, even, if she had no other choice. But when it turned into two days of living and breathing in close quarters with a man who had decided to awaken a long-dormant part of Penny with nothing more than a kiss against a cold, hard brick wall ...

Well, she was going crazy.

And it was her own fault.

Because with nothing else to do but sit and wait for some kind of word or sign from her handlers at The League, all she was left with were her thoughts. Since she wasn't the type to obsess over the things she *couldn't* change—like the fact that what should have been a simple transaction went to total shit in the blink of an eye—she was stuck going over every minute detail of what happened between her and Luca.

It was unexpected.

But she *liked* it.

He'd apologized.

She hadn't wanted him to.

Perhaps part of the problem was that she had gone years without any kind of physical intimacy with someone that she felt *anything* for on a personal level. Sex was a mechanical, chemical need that was easily fulfilled between humans, right? That, she could handle just fine and well. Except, apparently, when a man she had been attracted to for years decided to pin her against a wall, kiss the breath from her lungs, and touch her body with hands that promised they would learn every inch of her and enjoy doing it.

It wasn't so mechanical, then.

Definitely still chemical.

And she was stupid.

Stupid to focus on how she could still feel Luca's mouth against her own. Silken lips that made her feel *hungry*. Hands that grabbed just hard enough to wake up a need for more in the same way it spiked the part of her that was scared, too.

It lasted less than a minute and hadn't been anything more than a way to escape a bad situation. A distraction for their pursuers to give them a little bit more time to get to safety. That was what she kept telling herself but it was a lie.

He had been *hard* when he was pressed up against her; a natural reaction, maybe, but she didn't know any other man who got erections when they were seconds away from losing their life. And if his kiss had made her hungry, then he'd been ravenous. He hadn't *had* to touch her the way he did, or keep a hand on her like he didn't want to let go when the man finally opened the door, but he did.

And that was every reason why she kept obsessing over a single minute in her life that was already over. Something else she couldn't change, sure, but she wasn't capable of letting it go, either. Maybe because that one minute was something she had imagined time and time again when she was younger, stupider, and *broken*, but her imagination hadn't done it justice.

She was weak.

That's what it was.

Weak and *dumb,* and controlled by a part of her body that was practically useless to her at any other time.

It felt punishingly poetic that the easiest part of her old life to escape—a man she had felt nothing more than a young, girlish crush for—was the same thing that was now causing her more problems than she knew what to do with. In more than just the obvious ways, too. Or was that irony?

Penny didn't know.

It wouldn't help if she did.

"What are you doing up there?"

The question had Penny jerking back to the present in an instant. On top of the dresser, resting on her knees so that she could see out the small window, she was quite aware how she must look to Luca with the skirt of her dress hiked up around her hips so that she had more balance on the shitty furniture.

He probably had a partial view of her ass. Despite not wanting to feel embarrassed by that fact—it wasn't like her body hadn't been put on display before for various reasons—she still felt the blush creep up her throat into her cheeks.

More foolishness.

Every time he made a comment over the last two days that she could even slightly twist as suggestive, Penny did the same thing. Averted her eyes. Hid her face so that he couldn't see the pink in her cheeks. *Quieted.* At least then, she wouldn't make a fool out of herself. Because if she couldn't get this stupid attraction under control, then she would make sure he didn't know it existed in the first place.

Solid plan, her mind taunted. Another bitch in her life currently.

Giving one last look out the window—at nothing because there was nothing to see but the brick of a neighboring building—Penny sighed and turned away from the window. She refused to look at Luca when she climbed down from the dresser to slip on the heels she had kicked off to the floor.

"Checking," she muttered.

"For what?"

"Someone. *Anyone.*"

A sign that someone from The League had finally decided to show up and make her hellish existence better. Maybe one of her handlers walking down an alleyway to save her from stumbling over her words while she blushed like a schoolgirl and threw herself at a man that was nothing more than a problem to what should be most important in her life.

She told Luca *none* of that.

It wouldn't do any good.

"Your people?" Luca asked. "I doubt you're gonna see anything looking out that window. Except for maybe—"

"Waste of time, anyway," Penny interjected. "They'll find me when they want to."

And that was the simple fact of the matter. Not that she would explain why or how to Luca—the guy didn't need more fodder to his fire when it came to tracking her down. A chip in her upper left arm, about the size of a grain of rice, assured that when the coast was clear and her handlers were comfortable, they would come.

Without issue.

"The shower is open if you want it," Luca said.

She *should.* Two days without a bath or shower was just about her limit, honestly.

Penny lifted her head, ready to agree, and thank him for the information but the words caught in her throat at the sight of Luca standing in the doorway to their tiny room with nothing more than a towel hanging around his waist. He was tall—*lean*, but not lanky. Golden skin dusted with dark hair glimmered under the dim light in the room, and the droplets of water that still clung to his black hair said he'd barely even used that towel before coming back to their room.

No ink marred his skin.

A couple scars on his chest only added to the chiseled planes that made up a muscular torso. The bands of his arms, threaded with veins she wanted to trace with her fingertips, flexed when he tossed the pile of clothes to the foot of the bed. It had been easier to focus on ignoring her attraction when he had been doing nothing more than coming and going from their room, bringing back food, a pillow, and even a book when she asked for it. All *clothed.*

Now, she was going to have this image of him burned into the back of her eyeballs. No doubt, that wouldn't help her at all.

Why?

Why was he so beautiful?

It was unfair, really.

"You okay?" Luca asked when she remained silent.

No.

Not at all.

"Fine," Penny managed to utter. "I'm just gonna—"

"You know, if you wanted to show me your ass, you could have just done that. You didn't need to climb up there and wait for me to come back."

Penny blinked, her mouth falling open audibly. "*What?*"

That was not that she did.

Luca laughed, grabbing his shirt from the bed and tossing her a wink as he flipped open the fabric. "I'm kidding, Penny. Lighten up."

She was in control at all times. It was one of the few things her training at The League had afforded her that she was *most* grateful for. And yet, when it came to this man, it seemed like her control didn't exist at all.

"I gotta go," Penny said, walking past a confused looking Luca to head for the doorway. "I need a shower."

Maybe a drink, too.

"Penny, hey—"

"I'll be back."

When she felt like it.

Luca's sigh rang out behind her before he called, "Don't leave the building."

Right.

Even if she wanted to, she didn't have a choice but to stay. That was ninety percent of the damn problem. She couldn't get away from him, and she wasn't sure she wanted to. This couldn't possibly lead her to anywhere good.

· · ·

The shower did *nothing* for Penny. It certainly didn't help with her growing problem despite the fact that she couldn't even get the water to a bearably warm temperature. Cold showers were a joke even when it was unintentional. She did manage to snag a black tank top someone had left hanging from a makeshift clothesline in the hallway to throw on and with the skin-tight slip she wore under her dress to help conceal any weapons, it was like a whole new outfit.

Mostly.

She might return the top.

If she felt like it.

Penny found the bar Luca had mentioned on their first day after wandering a maze of halls for what felt like an hour. Attached to a kitchen where she was positive Luca had been getting their food from during their stay, the bar wasn't much to look at. But neither was the rest of the place, either. Mismatched tables, booths, and chairs were set up haphazardly to face a small platform where a singer was currently crooning into a microphone through a haze of smoke.

This place wasn't legal by any stretch of the imagination. That much was clear. It also served a purpose because she didn't think she had ever seen such a melting pot of people as the ones that lingered in the bar and kitchen.

She also found what served as the entrance. Not that it appeared that way. More like a nondescript door between two others where a man stood with a weapon at his hip, deciding who could and could not come inside which led directly into the bar.

Despite the strange atmosphere of the place, no one paid her any mind when she found a seat at a table near the back of the bar. With only the tank top and slip to cover her skin, her patchwork of scars was on clear display.

No one even looked her way.

They didn't care.

It made it easier for her to forget that she wasn't *trying* to blend in when she really didn't have to in the first place. How long had it been since she just … was?

Too long.

Maybe that was the general rule of the place. Don't ask, don't tell. If no one caused a problem, then someone wouldn't cause a problem with them. Penny liked that just fine.

Luca finally came to find—and join her at the table—when Penny was six drinks deep. Vodka soda wasn't her favorite alcohol to drink, but the place wasn't exactly equipped for the kinds of martinis she preferred. Simple would have to do.

She didn't even glance Luca's way when he slipped into the chair next to hers. At the other side of the room, the female singer crooned her way through a rendition of *Lana Del Rey's Heroin*. The song was decades old but the tune certainly fit the vibe of the place. And maybe even Penny's current mood.

Luca said nothing, but Penny couldn't help but fill the silence between them.

"I like this place," she admitted. "It's … different."

"Not the social standard?"

She shrugged. "Different."

His head turned a bit in the corner of her vision, telling her that he was now looking right at her and trying to decipher what she meant. He was free to do that all he wanted; she wasn't giving away the thoughts she kept locked up tight.

"Like you," he said, not even posing it as a question. "I'm sure you feel different, too. Maybe like you don't fit in with the typical crowd … it's not a place where you belong. Instead, you spend your time living in the undergrounds where people play at a new level of rules and only occasionally come out to blend in with the rest of the world when needed."

Christ.

Why did he have to be right?

"Yeah, well—"

He interrupted her mutter with a quiet, "I get it."

She did look at him, then, angling her body in the chair just enough that she could observe him from the side. He'd lost the leather jacket and hoodie, instead, now wearing his dark-wash jeans and the black shirt he'd been sleeping in since they arrived. At least, whatever soap he'd managed to find to use in the shower upstairs left him with a fresh, crisp scent. One she couldn't stop trying to inhale.

Another problem.

Perfect.

"I told Freddie we might be here a while longer," Luca said.

"*You* don't need to be here at all. In fact, you would make shit a lot easier for me if you do leave before someone finds—"

Luca sucked air through his teeth, jumping in to say, "Yeah, probably not."

"Why are you so …"

His head tipped her way, those shockingly intense green-blue eyes of his watching her like he was trying to dissect her. The shadows from the lack of lighting in the bar only hardened the lines of his handsome face even more. If there was a God, then he spent a little more time creating Luca.

Unfortunately for her.

"I'm not anything," Luca said, "and maybe that's the problem. I'm not all that different than how I used to be, Penny, but you … well, you're entirely new. I mean, *look at you.*"

She blinked. "I don't under—"

"I spent the last five years chasing after a ghost. I was trying to find someone who didn't exist anymore. Everything you are is not what you were, and that's *fine.* It's certainly for the better, but it took me a second to catch up to speed. Don't fault me."

"Is that … an apology?"

Because she wasn't sure.

Luca chuckled, the sound a sinful tease to her senses. "What would I be apologizing for, exactly?"

"I don't know. Finding me?"

"Nah, that was just my job. Anything else?"

Penny didn't reply.

What could she say?

Luca lifted one shoulder, saying, "There's your answer."

Penny rolled her eyes. "*Prick.*"

Maybe it was the alcohol doing stupid things to her already foolish brain, but when she found Luca looking over at her with the kind of smile that could make women swoon, a soft giggle escaped her mouth. The sound only made his gaze drop down to her lips while his smile dipped into an all too knowing smirk.

"We've got a problem," she told him.

Luca arched a brow. "Do we?"

"I think so. Starting with the fact you're an issue that's going to cause me even bigger problems if I don't get you under control. No matter how many times I tell, and *ask*, you to leave me alone, you won't. What happens if someone doesn't give you a choice in the matter?"

"The tracking you thing?" Luca shook his head. "*Again?* That's nothing."

She didn't think so. The man couldn't possibly know it but every second he spent around her put his life in danger. And not just him … his family and friends. Anyone who might cause issues for The League but especially those that became visible to the people she was hunting. Because if the monsters couldn't find her, then they would move onto the next best thing. People she cared about; anyone attached to her life that they believed would hurt her to lose.

She had a feeling Luca wouldn't care if she tried to explain. Five years of his life had been dedicated to finding her and bringing her home. If that wasn't an obsession, then she didn't know what was.

Did he even realize it?

That was the real question.

"What else would I be talking about?"

"I was thinking maybe that you realized I don't really see you like the same broken little girl I used to … and it fucked you up."

Penny swallowed hard. "Well—"

"*Penny.*"

She looked his way.

He hadn't looked away.

"What, Luca?" she whispered.

"It fucks me up, too."

"What do we do with that, then?"

He flashed his teeth in a grin. "Maybe this."

"What—"

He closed the distance between their chairs before she even knew what was happening. When his lips pressed against hers, there was no hesitation in Penny's mind before she answered his kiss back. His hands threaded into the loose waves of her white-blonde hair before finding her jaw. Every stoke of his lips against her own coaxed open her mouth until his tongue tangled with hers.

There she was.

Stupid, again.

Breathlessly dumb.

But *happy.*

All because he kissed her.

When he did finally pull away, Penny was left with more confusion than before. At least when she only had her own attraction to deal with, things were easier. Adding his to the mess made all of this far more complicated. Because it—*they*—couldn't be anything. Ever. Certainly not like this.

"I wanted to see," he murmured, his thumbs stroking the line of her jaw with a touch that sent heat spiraling throughout her body.

"See what?"

Her words were air.

He didn't seem to mind.

"If you wanted me to kiss you again."

Penny could only ask, "Did you figure it out?"

"I did."

And then he kissed her again. Penny let him. She *wanted* it.

15.

THE last thing Luca expected to find himself doing was *Penny.* So to speak. A part of him was still trying to reconcile the girl he remembered with the woman she had become in the years since he'd first met her. But it had become very apparent to him that it didn't matter when that time was already over, and he had to deal with the *now.*

And Penny *now?*

He wanted that.

Her.

More than he should—more than was okay, even.

He had done well to ignore it during their stay at Freddie's haven but with nothing else to do but look at Penny, or wander the halls of the large building and think, it kept leading Luca back to the same thing. Her.

It all came right back to her.

He shouldn't have kissed her the first time, but that could be excused as a needed requirement to get the two of them out of a bad situation. Except he kept thinking about it. The way her lips felt against his—how he wanted another taste and to touch her again. Until his fingers felt a phantom ache that didn't exist, and they itched with the need to trace the scars that covered her thighs and arms and even her chest while she slept in the small bed next to him.

Oh, he hadn't slept.

Not a fucking wink.

He'd been too busy staring at her.

"You're obsessed," she whispered against his lips.

Luca's heavy breath pulsed from his mouth to hers when he hovered over her where he had backed her against the hallway wall. Just outside their room. Another couple of feet and they would be safely out of view. Yet, when those words slipped past her trembling lips, swollen and pink from their kisses, he couldn't think about anything *but* what she said.

"How—"

"Me," Penny told him. "You're obsessed with me. Maybe the idea of me or this ghost of who I used to be, but still ... How could you not be? How long have you spent looking for even a hint of my existence? How many times have you talked about me, thought about me ... how many pictures and videos have you watched for even a glimpse of me? Am I in your dreams, Luca? Do I fill your thoughts when the day is quiet and no one is around? Do you think of me in a crowded room, too?"

God.

Every single one of her words hit him right in the fucking chest. Like they were punches she had thrown with the knowledge that their impact would take his breath away. It certainly didn't hurt like he thought maybe it should, but the weight was still heavy.

And hard to carry.

He wanted to deny it.

He *tried.*

"You don't know that," he muttered, watching her while his hands locked her wrists at both sides of her head. "You don't know any—"

"Am I your every waking thought? How many calls a day are dedicated to finding information about me? Have you ever dated in the last five years since you started this for Naz? Do you have a life at all outside of trying to find *me*? Or is it just … me?"

A slow, steady stream of air passed his lax lips as he desperately tried to find something—anything—to prove what she said wasn't true. Not because she seemed pleased or satisfied but rather, that she knew at all. That she could say it so easily, without malice, while it still managed to taunt him all the same.

But she wasn't wrong.

Here he was at thirty years old playing hide and seek with a ghost from his past, but the game had changed. Everything he used to want was inconsequential to *winning*. Because winning meant finding her and bringing her home to the people who loved her the most. He couldn't quite say that he was ready for the new rules—the game had clearly changed between them—but what choice did he have now?

"Luca," Penny murmured, "just say it."

He wanted to.

He *did.*

"So what if—"

"Because there's only one way this can end, and you know that. I'm going to disappear again. I have to. My job isn't done, and it might never be. And you, well, you're going to keep chasing me. Don't you want something else—something more with someone who … don't you want to *live*?"

He blinked.

Again with those targeted words that he couldn't deny or avoid.

"Why are you saying this?" he asked, stuck between the thumping pain in his heart, and his cock that had been hard from the second he kissed her again downstairs. "Why would you say these things to me *now*?"

Penny was a beautiful creature; it was impossible not to see all the reasons why when he was this close to her. The blue veins under the surface of her almost white skin. How the slight flush of pink traveled from her cheeks to her throat and even down under the tank top covering her chest. Without makeup, she looked like porcelain with blonde lashes and brows that framed the bluest eyes he had ever seen.

The curves that made up her body was a map he wanted nothing more than to learn with his tongue and his hands and his cock. She might have been damaged by her own hand—and by others, too—with scars he could see and even more that he couldn't, but she was still perfect.

A living, breathing *doll*.

Except she wasn't a doll.

She was right.

Until then, she hadn't been real to him in a way. The idea of her had been something he felt like he was trying to save for his friend and sister. Nothing less, and nothing more.

But then she was.

She was more.

"Because who else will?" Penny asked. "Who else knows the truth to tell you it, Luca?"

"*Stop it.*"

The force of his words matched the strength in his hands when he squeezed her wrists tighter against the wall and stepped closer. Crowding her space until their lips were a breath away and their noses touched.

She stared him down, though.

Unafraid.

He liked that, too.

Luca wished he didn't.

"Just stop—"

"No," she replied softly. "I won't. Ever. Because neither will you."

He hated that she was right. Even more, he hated that he didn't care because it made no difference to what he would do after this. She had to know it, too.

Luca didn't get the chance to tell Penny that, though, because in the next breath she was kissing him. Her lips locked against his as her fingernails dug into the sides of his hands almost painfully when his palms slid from her wrists to hold tight. His tongue flicked against the seam of her mouth, and when she opened to let him deeper, everything else faded away.

His ability to breathe.

Her words that *hurt*.

The hallway around them.

It all went away when he kissed her, letting go of her hands to drag his palms down the skin of her inner arms that felt like a patchwork from the multitude of scars. And yet, she was still as soft as silk, too. Her body arched into his, hiding nothing. Her thighs trembled when they opened to get more of him against her.

He gave her that, too, driving their bodies together like the two of them were teenagers getting their first taste of something sinful. Grinding against her until his balls ached with the need for more, and she was panting into his kiss almost ready to plead.

He doubted she would.

She didn't seem like the type to beg a man for anything, even her pleasure. Luca understood why and wouldn't try to make her … at least, not tonight. She could just take what she wanted from him instead, and he would be all too happy to give it to her.

"*Yo*—take that shit out of the hallway, or I'm getting Freddie's ass up here!"

Penny's teeth cut into Luca's lower lip at the same time the warning rang out from down the hall. Her hands froze against his chest where she had started to pull at his shirt like she was going to rip it right off. Her stare flicked up to his, the amusement dancing there held no shame or embarrassment … or control.

Like him.

All of this was just instinctual now.

A need.

"Hey, I said—"

"Fuck off," Luca snarled to the side.

He didn't look at the man—didn't even see who it was. All it took was the press of his hand against Penny's trim waist, and she slid to the side with him following right behind. She entered their room first, already pulling the tank top over her head before he had even closed the door with a slam that echoed. The button on his jeans snapped apart under his handling as she turned around.

They were two steps apart.

She closed it in a blink.

There was no softness in what came next. Their kisses stung, and his teeth left marks behind on her white skin. She gave back the same roughness she found in him, uncaring how he hissed when she yanked his shirt off before dragging her sharp nails down the expanse of his chest. When the slip of a skirt she wore fell to the floor around her heels, Luca let out a whistle.

"When did you take your panties off? How long were you walking around like that, Penny?"

She grinned, her black bra the only thing keeping any part of her body covered. He couldn't help but admire the sight of her when she took two steps back, stopping only when her legs hit the foot of the bed.

"Since my shower," she admitted.

"*Goddamn.*"

"We had to at least make it to the room, didn't we?"

Luca cocked a brow. "But did we?"

"Stop talking, Luca," she said, reaching up to unsnap the bra where the cups connected at the valley between her breasts, "and come fuck me."

So brazen.

Sure.

She knew what she wanted and that called to him more than anything else. There was nothing he found more attractive than that—shit, he got off on it, really.

The bra came apart and slid down her arms, discarded to the floor. In nothing but black heels, she stood at the foot of the bed and waited. Her entire life and story stared back at him, he knew. An hourglass figure that before it had even developed had been used and abused many times over. The scars she had cut into herself to chase away the pain. A grown woman who had finally grown into someone he didn't know at all.

But he wanted to.

God.

He wanted to know her.

"Now," Penny demanded quietly despite her firm tone, kicking off her heels and losing four inches of height instantly. Not that it mattered—her legs were still a work of art that he wanted to get wrapped around his head while he tasted the bare heaven between her thighs.

He wanted to keep staring—learning and appreciating. Committing her to his memory because hadn't she already warned him what would happen after this? What was inevitable? But he wouldn't waste time, either.

Luca would take what he could get; anything she was willing to give.

She reached for him when he stepped closer, the small space of the room closing around him as her hands slipped beneath his opened jeans. His mouth crashed against hers, tasting the heat on her tongue while her hands worked magic. She stroked him with one hand while her other pulled at his jeans until she had them down around his hips.

Close, they were chaotic.

Kisses that hurt and hands that ached. He couldn't get enough of her. No matter how many times he felt her skin under his hands, finding she liked a tight squeeze rather than a soft touch, he only wanted more.

Everything changed.

Fast.

Penny let his cock go just when his stomach had started to clench from the pressure she applied to his length with every tug. He barely had time to process the loss before she had twisted him around and his back hit the bed. For a seemingly little thing, she had strength.

Or she knew how to move.

Luca palmed her hips when she climbed on top of him. The flash of her sex had his mouth watering before she yanked his jeans and boxer-briefs low enough for his cock to spring free. Then she was grinding against him, the wet slit of her pussy a hot heaven to his senses. He held her too tight, he knew it. He couldn't breathe with her rocking on him like she was. The almost feral sounds that clawed their way out of his chest wasn't something he recognized.

"How long's it been?" she asked, leaning down so her mouth hovered over his. "How long has it been since somebody made you come, Luca? Could I do it like this—just rubbing on you, do you want me to?"

Internally, the answers came too easily, but he couldn't form the words. Penny's tongue swept her bottom lip while one of her fingers traced a line down his clenching jaw. Every swivel of her hips while the satisfaction in her stare sharpened had his ecstasy skyrocketing. He urged her own by pulling her body harder against his, feeling how her wetness coated his dick more and more.

"Could I?" she asked again, breathless and shaking.

"After I taste you."

That had her stilling.

Lifting a bit, too.

Luca held her tight, refusing to let go of her gaze or her body when he murmured, "Let me taste you, Penny."

"I don't … I nev—"

He flexed his hands, pushing her higher until she straddled his chest. "*Let me.*"

She did, letting him adjust her until she was resting overtop his face, and he had the best view of her wet cunt. Just inches from his mouth, he could already smell the tartness of her sex and arousal; he could see it, too, glistening on pink flesh and a slit that clenched when a groan of approval pressed past his lips.

He tasted her while he watched her up above; that first lick flooding his taste buds and making his mouth water. She *shuddered.* From her shoulders to the tips of her toes against the mattress. His second lick started at the soft fleshiness of her pussy right up to the tight bud of her clit.

There, he sucked.

Hard, long.

"*Jesus.*"

Her exclamation came with fingernails that dug into his scalp, pulling at the strands of his hair like she might rip them right out of his head. He didn't mind. Something was new for her in this—he could tell. At least, in a willing way.

That only made him hotter.

Out of control, really.

Like the rest of her, once he had indulged in a single taste, it just wasn't enough. His fingers dug into the firm roundness of her ass while he feasted. On her cunt, the flavor of her, and every little sound she made. It was all a drug. He wanted so much more. Another hit of her.

He found that hit when he found the rhythm she responded to best, rapid snaps of his tongue under the hood of her clit that had her hips rocking into his mouth for more. She seemed surprised at how fast the orgasm came on, her eyes flying wide and nailing into his down below as her body tensed and the low, keening whine passed her parted lips.

She whispered his name.

"Luca."

It was the best thing he ever heard.

Almost.

He decided it was the second-best sound when even as she hadn't stopped shaking, she slid down his body with a demand for, "More—make me come again."

Not *I want to.*

Not that she would do it.

She wanted it from him.

He was being stupid, and he knew it because he thought about nothing but being buried inside of her. Even as they helped each other from what remained of their clothes, the last thing on his mind was being safe.

Yeah.

Stupid.

He also didn't care when she slid down his length and leaned in for a kiss. With the taste of her still on his lips, she licked it from his mouth while he filled her full. The tightness of her cunt, wet and hot around him, drove Luca to the edge of insanity in a split second.

The long length of her white hair fell like a curtain over her bouncing tits with every lift and lower of her body. He found her hands with his own, weaving their fingers together when she straightened up and watched him down below.

She was still clenching tight from her first orgasm; his cock worked into those tight muscles. He kept her arms high over her head with one hand while his other palmed her throat. She didn't shy away from that, either, and then he could really pound into her.

Those rising moans …

Every broken cry …

It was because of him.

Luca knew it shouldn't be—this wasn't what he was supposed to be doing with Penny. He couldn't even begin to fathom how he would tell his friend what he had done here.

He also didn't care.

Not in that moment.

How could he when he had *this?*

• • •

"Success," Luca said as he slipped back into the room with a bottle of unopened vodka in hand. "I had to bribe the guy who handles the liquor but—"

"I always wanted to come back."

The door closed under Luca's hand, but he didn't move away from it. Instead, he watched Penny from where she sat in the middle of the bed. The thin blanket pooled at her waist, doing nothing to hide the nakedness of her upper body. She didn't seem to mind as she fingered the edge of the blanket, her brow drawn down in her thoughts.

"Back here, you mean?"

Because that's what he hoped she meant.

"I *wanted* to," she said, making him hear what she was trying to say. "But it wasn't supposed to happen. Or at least, that's what I was always told. I gave up something to give something back ... I know it doesn't make sense to you. Maybe you want to understand—"

"All you have to do is tell me."

Penny shook her head. "Not when that means doing more damage, Luca. Not when it might mean ruining everything that's got me to this point. I'm *so* close."

Anger at not knowing what she was trying to tell him rushed out of him when he snapped, "To what?"

She didn't reply.

He should have expected that.

"It won't matter, will it?" she asked.

Crossing the room, he tossed the small pint of vodka he'd managed to snatch from the downstairs to the bed. "Depends."

"If I ask you to stop again—if I tell you everything depends on you going away and staying there. It won't matter. You can't."

"I promised my friend to find you."

"And you *have.*"

"But you're not where you should be, Penny," he said. "And you know that, too."

"I don't belong anywhere now. I can't."

"Tell me you don't miss them. Say you don't give a shit about the godson you left behind. Open that fucking mouth of yours and at least *lie.* If you can't even do that, then why would I stop? I've gotten this far—"

"But you won't get more."

He didn't understand.

He also knew she wouldn't explain.

Penny looked up from the blanket, observing while he lingered at the end of the bed. There was something soft in her stare, but he found something else there, too. A longing, maybe. But for what, he didn't know.

"Come back to bed," she said. "At least there's this. We can have this."

Right.

For now.

16.

BEFORE, any physical intimacy Penny willingly had with a man would end the second it was over, and she got what she wanted from it. She didn't linger; there was nothing to stay for, really. She expected her partners to do the same and not demand anything more.

Everything was easier that way.

It worked.

Except with Luca ...

While he seemed determined to remain with her until she forced his hand—and she couldn't leave when she was ordered to wait for The League's signal—she also didn't mind his company. She was, however, too prideful to admit that the days following her falling into bed with him passed quicker because he was there.

Because she couldn't leave him alone.

It was just ... too good.

And wasn't Penny allowed to indulge herself just once?

Naked and unbothered next to her in the bed, she could feel Luca's gaze watching her, but she refused to turn her head his way. Instead, she focused on the cracked plaster of the ceiling over top the bed while his fingers tapped a soothing beat to the inside of her elbow. Before long, she recognized the familiar tapping. It was like the notes he was pretending to play had started to take shape in her mind, ringing out with actual sound in her brain though no one else could hear it but her.

The pianist in her was still alive and well. Her need for music had never dimmed as much as it just became secondary to everything else in her life over the years.

"Rosalynn's third stanza of what she called *The Nineth Composition*," Penny said. "She played it in Australia at every show, right?"

Out of the corner of her eye, she saw Luca's grin. "She did. I'm not very good at piano, but I can at least play a little ... if I go slow."

That had her snorting.

"What good is playing slow?"

She felt him shrug as he shifted on the bed to rest his head in his hand, propped up higher so now she couldn't pretend like she was unable to see him. While her body was made up of scars that told a tale she would rather not, his was not the same. A beautiful canvas of golden, tanned skin and a muscular form that deserved to be appreciated. There was something decadent about running her hands over his chest and arms; feeling his dark dusting of hair and the way his bands of muscles jumped at her touch like he needed it.

She held back from reaching over to do just that—it would only lead them into another sweaty mess of tangled limbs, and she was trying to show some self-control.

A joke, honestly.

She wanted to fuck again and again. As soon as they were done. Day after day. Night in and night out. Self-control?

What was that?

"You still play?" he asked.

Penny smiled. "Rarely."

"But you *do*."

The lump that formed in her throat was almost impossible to swallow. It was only there because of how easily she wanted to tell him the truth about the piano and why she played so infrequently now. He made her want to talk; that was dangerous.

Still, Penny said, "I have a Baby Grand I can use whenever I want, but I don't compose anymore. Not my own pieces, I mean. I haven't played a show since ... before I tried to kill myself when I was sixteen. I don't think—"

She stopped talking when his fingers drifted lower on her arm, tracing the lines upon lines that made up her skin. Faded scars that had long turned white and the few, deeper ones that were still a pinkish-red tone. Most were raised and the ridges couldn't be missed from how she had cut into the same lines again and again.

"That still a thing?" Luca asked in a murmur.

"What?"

"Suicide. Attempts or otherwise. Curious."

He sounded like he was telling the truth. His expression gave nothing away to say he was lying or overthinking.

Penny flicked a strand of white-blonde hair away from her face, muttering, "Considering I've had suicidal ideations since I was too young to even understand what I was thinking, that's just a part of my brain. I'm wired like that, you know? Wired wro—"

"Not wrong, Penny."

She laughed sharply. "You sound like Cree. Wanna shrink my head, too? They've all taken a shot at it, but I can't promise it will get you anywhere."

Luca's expression didn't change to say anything she said interested him. No doubt, the man was soaking it all in, though. Planning how he might be able to use it in the future when he found himself chasing after her again.

"And no," she added quieter. "All those attempts were brought on by circumstance and situations at the time. Waking up every day and thinking *what would it be like if I died today* isn't quite the same as making an active plan and trying to see it through, Luca."

"Hmm."

"What?"

"How many times?"

That had Penny frowning. "Why?"

"Curious."

"About my suicide attempts?"

Luca cleared his throat. "About everything. *Anything.*"

"You shouldn't ask—"

"Why, because you actually want to answer? Because you like to talk to me as much as you like fucking me?"

Penny dragged in a hard breath, hating how fast he had hit the nail right on the head. "Luca ..."

"It's only fair. You threw some baggage at my feet to unpack. I'm just handing some back, Penny."

Right, well—

Before she could finish her thought, let alone reply to Luca, a knock echoed on the door of their room. In the many days that they had spent in the underground haven, not once had someone came to their room. Not even Freddie.

Luca passed Penny a look, asking, "Do you want me to get it?"

"I think I can handle it."

"Just saying. The offer is there."

Mmhmm.

If there was anything this man should know about her by now, it was that she could certainly take care of herself when the situation called for it. Penny was far from helpless. She would never be the damsel in need of saving.

Wasn't her style.

She lived that life once.

It was enough.

Pushing out of the bed when the knock echoed again, she grabbed Luca's shirt from the floor and pulled it over her head. Punching her arms through the sleeves, she gave him a look over her shoulder, pointedly.

With a roll of his eyes, he covered his nakedness with the blanket. Although it did nothing to hide his sexiness, or the way he stared at her like he wanted her back in the bed as soon as possible. *Damn.* She felt the same.

"Better?" he asked.

"Barely," she replied.

Luca grinned. "*Right.*"

The prick.

He was too cocky for his own good. And she liked it.

Too much.

That was the problem.

Refusing to let her thoughts dance near *that* danger, Penny reached for the doorknob while she pointed her finger at Luca in warning. He made her stupid; not that he could possibly know it. She made dumb choices with him involved.

Even now.

She had opened the door and didn't even look to see who was waiting out in the hallway until she heard a male chuckle.

"Did I interrupt?" came a voice she knew.

Not well.

She *did* know it, though.

"Renzo," Penny said, facing their guest.

In the hallway, Renzo Zulla leaned a bit to the side, staring past her at the man in the bed. She hadn't seen the older League assassin in a couple of years. He'd come in to help train a new recruit a little while back, but she was overseas during that time. Now based and living in New York, it made sense for Cree—or Dare—to send him to find her.

"Well, did I interrupt?" Renzo asked again.

Penny opened her mouth to speak, but Luca beat her to the punch as he reached for a pack of cigarettes and a lighter he had somehow managed to find over the past day. "Not at all, man. What's up?"

She sighed, ignoring the gazes that came her way from both men. It was obvious what the two of them had been doing before Renzo came along. She wasn't going to indulge these two idiots by saying anything about it. All one needed to do was look at what she was wearing and Luca's *lack* of clothes.

Renzo smiled, clearly amused. "Penny, when you have a minute ... I'll be downstairs. We need to have a chat."

As she thought.

Her time with Luca was undoubtedly coming to an end.

● ● ●

"I didn't realize my invitation extended to your ... friend," Renzo said, eyeing the man who followed behind Penny when she approached the table inside the bar.

Luca grinned, passing the two of them by as he pointed at the booth a few feet away. "I'll just be over there. Listening, of course."

Renzo's brow lifted.

Penny shrugged. "Hazard of my current situation. He kind of got stuck here with me. For the moment, anyway."

"Mmm." Renzo pointed at the chair opposite to his at the table. "Sit." She did.

Two glasses of water appeared from the man who served drinks like Renzo had planned for that. Penny didn't touch hers while the man across from her downed half of his in ten seconds. She could get water anytime; right now, she wanted news.

"Well?" she demanded.

Renzo sat the glass down, glancing her way. "It's like Dare suspected. Someone is onto you. The system The League has been using to track and dismantle members of The Elite is the same thing they're doing to you right now. Every move you make in any capacity, they're turning it around to their benefit. They had the chance to draw you out because you had already attached yourself to Elijah Smithenson with his murder, and so the bait was set."

Penny's jaw ached. She really needed to unclench her teeth before she broke a molar. Easier said than done, though.

"And that means what—"

"That we can safely assume any move you make after this latest attack will undoubtedly provoke another at some point," Renzo interjected. It was clear he already knew her question, and the answer before she could even get it out. Obviously the man had been well briefed before he arrived to chat with her. No doubt, that was part of the reason why The League had taken so many days to track Penny down at her current location. "And things will have to change because of that."

She wasn't willing to accept that. They were too close to finally coming to a head with the wealthy, powerful pedophile ring to stop now because shit was getting dangerous.

"It was a one-time thing," Penny replied, shrugging. "A stupid mistake on my part. I got into my feelings about what I thought was a situation I could help. So, we don't do that again. Seems simple."

"Highly unlikely—"

"We're careful," she snapped, her irritation spilling over at the very idea that her handlers—or even her boss—might call the entire plan off. She had worked *years* for this. Suffered her entire life to finally end this hell. "And we can be more careful. Make it harder to trace me. Use others in my place for a time. Things *can* be done."

Renzo observed her in silence. He was just a messenger, she knew. One shouldn't kill those, but she was seriously considering it at the moment. Some things just couldn't be helped.

At Penny's left where he sat with nothing in front of him, watching the scene unfold, Luca spoke up with, "If I could track you down, even by shit luck in some cases, then someone else can, too, sweetheart. Someone with more money, control … *access*. You should consider—"

"Fuck off. Don't talk on something you don't know."

Out of the corner of her eye, she saw Luca's brow arch.

"Ouch," he murmured.

She would have apologized.

Except *no*.

He didn't understand what was on the line. The guy didn't have a single clue how much was at stake now.

"He has a point, even if you're unwilling to listen," Renzo said quietly. "The plan from here on out is for you to move a lot less than you have been—don't be seen. At all. Nothing is to be done with your name, moniker, or otherwise, attached. Or The League. Not until the situation is under control and a better assessment has been done where all parties involved can make an educated decision on continuing with the plan. As of now, the plan is off—"

"*No*."

Renzo dragged in a heavy breath.

Penny swallowed hard. "No, we're finally making progress here. It would be stupid to give them time to protect themselves further than they already have. They're *weak*. Now is the best time to finish it entirely."

"Dare has made the call, Penny. Your directive is clear—if you don't follow orders, then you know the risk you're taking. Beyond just the consequences you'll take from The League and your boss, you'll put everyone who can be connected to you in danger."

Luca.

Nazio.

Roz.

Little Cross.

Any Donati.

Probably Luca's family, too.

She knew it.

And still …

Nothing was simple.

This was also *for* them.

17.

Luca

LUCA was finally the fly on the wall in Penny's life, gathering more information by the second to connect every dot he had ever missed, but he wasn't sure that he liked it. Especially while the conversation between her and Renzo continued at the table. He wasn't stupid—the few things that had slipped from Penny over the time they were together added into what he already knew, and now piled onto the details Renzo gave about the situation … it didn't take a rocket scientist to figure things out.

He could put two and two together.

This wasn't good.

At all.

Penny also didn't seem to care.

"So, what you're saying is The League is going to force my hand one way or another," Penny said, "because if a simple order isn't going to make me follow along, then the subsequent threat will?"

Renzo sighed. "You know it's not like that."

"What is it fucking like, then?"

"Dare and Cree—"

"Have no bone in this fight but *money.* The money they get for every successful job I do, and you know it. Were you any different, Renzo?"

The man at the other side of the table from Penny didn't blink a lash at her growing anger. "They warned me this might happen."

Penny's brow dipped. "Excuse me?"

"This," Renzo said, gesturing between the two of them. "That you would put up a fight about everything. They planned for that, too."

Now, it was Luca's turn to worry about what he was hearing. He managed to stay quiet at his table but only because he didn't think speaking up would help the situation at all when he still wasn't sure what the entire situation *was,* to begin with.

One thing was clear, though.

Every single move Penny had made up until that moment had been done with a purpose for her work and little else. It was obviously the one and only thing that kept her moving. The very idea that someone planned to shut her down—even for a time—was too much for her to handle.

He supposed if the past five years of her life had revolved solely around hunting the same kind of monsters that had hurt her, it would be horrifying for someone to say they were going to back off. Allowing those same monsters to continue hurting others.

No wonder Penny had been able to pinpoint his obsession in finding her with such cruel precision. She wasn't any different from him at the end of the day; her reason for doing so was the only major change from his own.

"And because they figured this is what would happen when I came to deliver to you the news," Renzo continued saying, dragging Luca from his thoughts before they could spiral further. "Your handlers have arranged a private jet by your boss's demand—"

"Who's the boss, exactly?" Luca asked.

Speaking up before he could help himself.

Neither answered. In fact, they didn't even look his way. If the small bit of information he had gathered on The League was true—their practices and members were infamous for being difficult to track or infiltrate; his work trying to find Penny proved both to be correct—then getting the name of the person pulling *all* of Penny's strings would be impossible.

Assassins trained by The League were not owned by the organization but rather, whoever delivered them to their training. There were also rumors of auctions where assassins fresh out of the program were sold to the highest bidder to do whatever they wanted. Penny's situation could be either of those things—or something else entirely.

He doubted she would tell him even if he asked.

Renzo continued speaking to Penny as though Luca hadn't interrupted in the first place, explaining, "At the moment, considering everything that's happened, they all think removing you from the state and taking you back to Nevada is the best choice. The *only* choice."

"It's not the only—"

"It is," the man interjected, shrugging like nothing she said would make a difference. "You'll be better protected where The League has more control and resources. Once Dare and Cree are satisfied with the new plan— whatever that might be—then, you can go from there. So far, you've done well by going underground like you have, but now they want you to do that at headquarters. Or at least, somewhere within their reach. I'm sure you understand."

Despite her earlier anger, Penny reverted to a cold demeanor in a blink when she stood from the table and replied, "No, I *don't* understand."

Without another word, she stepped out from behind the table and shoved the chair in with a rough hand. She didn't even glance over her shoulder as she walked away, sending Luca to his feet to follow after her.

The man at the table held up a hand, stopping him when he said, "Let her go. Penny has always handled her issues far better when she's given the opportunity to do so alone."

Luca wasn't sure he believed that—no one wanted to be alone. Hadn't Penny spent enough time without the comfort of people who cared about her?

Nevertheless, with the chance to speak to the familiar man *without* Penny close enough to hear his questions, he couldn't pass up the chance. Instead of retaking his previous seat, he sat down in the one Penny had exited. Folding his arms over his chest, he observed the man staring him down.

"Renzo," Luca murmured.

The man cocked a brow. "What about it?"

"Renzo *Zulla*. Husband of Lucia Marcello—daughter of the former Marcello crime family underboss. Niece to the previous boss and cousin to the *current* man sitting in the seat, correct?"

Renzo's jaw tightened. "You know, when people start naming names in my personal life, I tend to take that as a threat."

"Cut the shit," Luca returned. "I recognize you. I'm sure you know who I am, too. Our connections intermingle."

"And that means what to me, exactly?"

A lot of things.

Or possibly nothing at all.

Luca figured … *nothing ventured, nothing gained.* It was a motto he could get on board with for his current situation. Penny wasn't telling him shit about her work or the people pulling the strings. Nothing he hadn't learned on his own. There was a chance he wouldn't get anything from Renzo either, even with their mutual connections on the table as encouragement, but he wouldn't know if he didn't at least try.

"I heard your boss came from the Marcello family," Luca said, smirking when Renzo's gaze darkened. "Is that where hers came from, too? Is someone from that side of the city pulling her strings and calling her moves?"

The silence grew between the two. It continued long enough to tell Luca that the other man wasn't going to feed into the conversation more than he had to.

Then, Renzo leaned forward, resting his elbows on the table and clasping his hands together, never moving his gaze from Luca's when he said, "I'm not sure what your business is with Penny—other than being a pest for her handlers when she's trying to work—but it would be wise for you to mind your business. Before you become a problem for someone who doesn't care about making you a sacrifice in this game."

"People keep telling me to back off," he noted, nodding to himself, "but every time I don't listen, I keep finding myself right where I need to be."

"Then, you're a fool with a suicide complex."

Not at all.

Luca pointed at Renzo, his fingers forming the shape of a gun. "*And* I'll be following along to Nevada. Just a heads up."

That had Renzo laughing.

"I don't think so, man."

"That's funny."

"What is?" Renzo asked.

"That you think any of you have a choice at this point. If I was only a pest for The League before where Penny was concerned, imagine the hell I can cause them now. The things I know … what I've seen, well, it could make a big problem."

"See, and that's where the suicide complex comes in. They *will* kill you before they let you close enough to do anything, Luca."

It was Penny's approach, and her voice that stopped him from replying when she said, "No, I think he's right. Luca will have to come along with me now. Better we can control what he's doing and where he's doing it than letting him run wild."

Renzo glowered.

Luca just smirked.

"See," he said. "She knows."

He had to be smug about it on the outside. A rule he had learned long ago was that any show of weakness would be manipulated in their life. He wouldn't give anything for Renzo to use against him or pass along to someone else, even if that something was just his worries about the unknowns ahead of him.

Of *everything*.

Would going to Nevada cause a problem? Probably. In more ways than anyone knew.

What was he going to tell Naz? As it was, he'd already been underground and unreachable for a week. He was busy, sure, but not so much so that his best friend or family didn't hear from him for days at a time. How much longer was this going to take?

It didn't matter.

Luca would lie if he had to—it was the only way he might be able to keep this charade up and see where it would end. Hopefully, with Penny coming home to the people who missed and needed her. Or at the very least, returning to their lives in some way. He could justify lying to his sister and Nazio—and anyone else that got in his way—if it meant succeeding in his goal.

Or …

That's what Luca would keep telling himself.

"Well," Penny said, slapping her hands at her sides and giving Renzo a pointed look, "when are we leaving?"

• • •

"Could I get you a drink or any snacks—"

"You can get the fuck out of my face," Penny snapped.

Her harsh words and the squeaky, unintelligible reply from the single flight attendant on the private jet had Luca turning away from the beautiful view beyond the porthole window. Three hours into their trip, and Penny had clearly hit her limit of patience and tolerance for the day.

It wasn't the first time she had been nasty to the woman who was only meant to help them throughout the flight. She even brushed off the pilot when they first boarded the jet. The man had only wanted to introduce himself which was standard.

At first, Luca blamed Penny's worsening mood on the fact this was happening at all when she had made it clear that she didn't want to return to Nevada. Not if it meant being put into lockdown while other plans were pushed aside. But as she unbuckled her seat belt and clamored across the aisle to snap shut the port window for the plush seats next to theirs, he wondered if it might be something else.

"Do you want me to close mine, too, or …?"

Penny glanced his way, but not at the window. "If you wouldn't mind."

He closed it. "You're scared of flying."

It wasn't even a question.

Penny exhaled hard. "A lot of my bad memories usually start with me getting on a fucking plane. I was a toddler, flown to Asia to deliver my virginity to a businessman with a taste for *babies*. Do you know what the contract said? My father kept it."

Luca's stomach twisted.

She didn't notice his discomfort.

"No, what?"

Penny shrugged. "Any physical damage—say a *tear*—would be corrected before I was returned. And it was. Wouldn't want to ruin the goods completely. It couldn't be sold again, right?"

"Jesus—"

"At five, I was flown to Cuba for a set of videos they filmed with a bunch of blonde-haired, blue-eyed girls and boys. We were the ones bringing in big money for the ring at the time. They wanted to get all they could out of it. Those videos were still making the rounds until I was eighteen, and someone with an ounce of talent with the dark web finally started pulling shit down. Of course, that means nothing for the creeps who still have their own files to jack off to, you know?"

"Penny—"

"I can keep going."

Luca frowned when she met his gaze. "I know, I'm sorry."

"Do you—do you *really* know?"

Sort of.

In details, mostly.

The experience was a whole other matter. He could sympathize and apologize, but he would never truly know what that had been like for Penny. The horrors of it affected him because he wasn't an unfeeling monster, but it was also a reality that hadn't been his own.

"Not really," he replied, "not like you do. No one will ever know the things you know because only you lived that life."

"Wrong," she whispered. "There are thousands of girls out there just like me. And little boys, too. You put one bastard down that hurts these kids, and three more get smarter about the way they do business, Luca. Because that's what it is. A multi-billion-dollar-a-year *business*. Children are the product they sell. And they're treated like it, too. They don't see little kids with broken souls. They just see something they want to fuck."

How should someone reply to that?

Luca didn't have the first clue.

"But yeah," Penny said, chewing on her bottom lip and offering a hesitant smile, "I'm also scared of flying because I don't like being thousands of feet in the air inside a tin can."

"Helpless."

Her blue eyes flicked away.

Not for long.

"You don't like being *helpless*," he said when her gaze found him again. "And so you've done almost everything you can to make sure that never happens again."

Penny waved two fingers almost dismissively. "And yet, here I am being exactly that."

"Because you're on a plane?"

"No," she muttered, "because they're going to fuck everything up."

"Who—The League?"

"Everybody." Penny looked away, her hands clutching to the armrests of the white leather seats when the plane jumped from a bit of turbulence. Seeing her knuckles whiten the tighter she gripped the seat, Luca reached over to unlock one of her hands with his own. Wordlessly, he wove their fingers, keeping their palms tight, so she could at least have some sense of support. He didn't acknowledge the way her hand trembled in his. Lower, she added, "And anyone else who gets in my way."

Did that include him?

If that was the case, then Luca wasn't sure how to settle the things he wanted and needed from Penny with hers.

Was he helping?

Or hurting?

109

Luca didn't ask.
Couldn't.
He feared the answer.

18.

Penny

"YOU knew that was going to be a problem."

"Good to see you alive and well, too, Cree," Penny said to her handler. "How was my trip to New York? Not bad. Almost got killed— unfortunately, Chase did end up with a couple of bullets in his back. But like Dare would say ... a hazard of the job. A little help from my problem here," she added, jerking a thumb in Luca's direction, "and everything was fine until you guys finally decided to show up and demand I leave. All in all, nothing incredible. What about you?"

Steadfast and unbothered by her attitude, Cree stood at the end of the complex's hallway with his arms folded over his broad chest. He might have talked to her, but his gaze nailed to the man at her side.

Luca.

"You *were* forewarned," Penny said. "By Renzo, I assume. Because there was no way in hell he would keep something like my new friend off the record. Right?"

Cree frowned. His one and only show of emotion as his attention moved to Penny with a slowness that spoke of his displeasure without needing to say a thing. "Of course, but forgive us for thinking you would have enough sense to lose the problem before we had to do it for you. That was the agreement before, wasn't it?"

"I always love when people talk about me when I'm right there," Luca said, stuffing his hands deep into the pockets of his jeans like he was conversing with old friends. "It's funny how everyone who does it thinks that I can't hear them. I have ears. They work perfectly fine."

That didn't make things better.

Cree's jaw flexed when he muttered, "You weren't invited to this conversation in the first place. Excuse my ignorance for keeping you out of it all the same."

"All right," Penny said, putting up a hand. "Restart for a second. I wasn't given much of a choice but to bring him along, okay? At least like this, with him here, we have control of *one* problem on our hands. Think about it."

Luca turned her way.

Slightly.

Subtly.

She could feel his gaze burning into her with questions right on the tip of his tongue. He was also a smart enough man to keep them inside his own mind. *For now.* It wasn't that he hadn't given her a choice entirely because *she* agreed to bring him along to Nevada. And if she really wanted to lose Luca, she could without trouble.

But it was better to have him in view.

He was also …

On her side.

Maybe he hadn't said as much, but he didn't have to. Penny knew it. At the moment, she wasn't sure who else would have her back if she needed it but chances were, Luca was one she could count on. His only motive for being anywhere near her *was* her. He didn't care about the rest, and she would be stupid not to see that for what it was.

Or use it.

If needed, she thought.

Cree let out a heavy sigh, eyeing the man beside Penny before he finally said, "Well, keep in mind that someone else in this building has already decided how he wants this problem to end, Penny. I didn't know you to be the type who dragged innocents into something they had no business being involved with in the first place."

"I'm not innocent," Luca returned.

Even though he shouldn't.

"We know exactly who you are, Luca Puzza. And your father and mother … your sister, her husband and their child, even. How's his first year in the private academy going, anyway? Our Sisters of Perpetual Sorrow—quite a name for an educational facility, isn't it? I'm sure the students of the faculty appreciate the irony. Then again, what would I know? My education never happened within the sanctity of four walls."

Luca tensed.

Penny didn't hesitate to reach over and grab his wrist to keep him from doing anything else he might be considering. Like moving forward or even voicing a threat that he couldn't take back. Cree was testing him—he might not know it or see it for what it was—but she did.

"Enough," she told Cree.

"He should know," the Native man returned, "that this is not a game and even if it were … we would always win."

"You made your point."

"But did I?"

Penny squeezed Luca's wrist, and leaned closer to murmur, "It's fine, I promise."

"Not sure a word is worth much here," he replied.

Well …

He wasn't entirely wrong.

"Back to the task at hand," Cree said from the other end of the hallway, "I assume your ... new friend can make himself comfortable? You'll rejoin him shortly, Penny. You have other things to attend to upstairs."

Right.

Dare.

Should be fun.

• • •

Dare didn't turn to greet Penny when she first entered his office but that wasn't anything unusual. Instead, he faced the massive screens that covered the entire wall behind his desk. Split into several mini views of the security cameras, they panned different sections of the complex, but he only seemed to be watching one in particular.

Luca.

"Look at that," Cree muttered beside her. "He managed to find the music room."

"*I* allowed him to. Better the enemy you know than the one you don't," Dare replied. All she needed was the tone to know he was pissed and balancing on the edge. The tension in his shoulders when he shook his head was a pretty good indicator, too. "Otherwise, he was just wandering halls and checking doors. He shouldn't *be* here at all."

"Quite aware, Dare. You shouted so loud when they first arrived that I'm positive anyone inside the complex right now heard it and knows he's here."

"I've had just about all of your smart ass comments that I can take today, Cree."

"Fair enough," Cree returned.

"But *you*."

Dare swung around all at once, the scowl etched into his face looked deep enough to stick permanently. He pointed a finger at Penny like it was supposed to mean something to her, but she only stared back, unaffected.

"Yes?" she asked.

"We have enough problems on our hands without *you* adding more to it for us to handle," he said, arching a brow as though he expected her to deny it. "And what did you do? Exactly that, Penny. You created another mess for me to clean. You know what I should do? I should have the man killed and buried out there in the desert. That would solve everything."

Her heart dared to stutter in her chest, skipping a beat and clenching painfully at the very idea this might not end the way she had hoped it would by bringing Luca here.

Dare didn't make threats.

Not ones he wouldn't keep.

It was that reason alone Penny was quick to say, "No, you won't."

"Excuse me?"

Two pairs of eyes drifted her way, their curiosity and disbelief burning brightly. She wasn't willing to rehash her previous conversation with Cree from downstairs, but she also didn't think she had to. The clench of Dare's jaw was enough to tell her that he had probably already heard it through one of his many cameras *and* knew she was right.

If he wanted Luca dead, it would be done.

Undoubtedly.

"There are at least a dozen members inside The League's complex at any given time," Penny said, shrugging. "Coming and going ... doing whatever the fuck you want them to do when they're not out on a job. If you wanted my companion dead, then we wouldn't be having this conversation, and he wouldn't be tuning the piano right now."

That comment had both men looking at the screens. Sure enough, Luca had opened the Baby Grand and already had a little box of tools they kept beneath the piano opened in front of him while he leaned over the side to work. Despite being alone in an unfamiliar place, one that felt like danger the second a person stepped inside the building, he didn't seem very concerned about his predicament.

He was either crazy.

Or ... something else entirely.

Penny didn't know, but she would be foolish to say a part of her didn't like it. Because she did.

"Someone would already be moving his corpse while you told me it was inevitable. Am I wrong?" she asked.

Dare openly glared.

He didn't deny her words, though.

Quietly, Cree told her, "*I* requested that he step back and try to handle the Luca situation in another way. For you."

That was surprising.

Penny didn't show it.

"Downstairs, you acted like—"

"Like you disobeyed orders and instructions," Cree interjected, "because you did. It's the whys that interest me more, Penny. I'm just not sure you're willing to discuss those reasons quite yet."

Well ...

She changed direction.

What was the point of this conversation, anyway?

"Are you sure the meeting in Hell's Kitchen was a trap set to draw me out?" she asked Dare.

"Without question."

"And why wasn't it caught?"

Dare scrubbed a hand down his face, the frustration rushing back to his features in a blink. "Because your feelings got in the way and I seem to indulge the emotional needs of my people instead of telling you all to shove it up your fucking ass—"

"Dare," Cree spoke up, not unkindly.

"It's *true!*" Anger exploded from the normally cold man, his red blazer unbuttoning from the force of his arms flying outward wildly. "We all *knew* she wouldn't be able to turn her back on the idea that a girl needed help, and we fed her right into the mouth of a *wolf.* We lost a damn good member of this organization because one of us wasn't willing to send her on that job alone. All because not a single one of you wanted to look at her and tell her no. *She* is not a child. The rest of them, they're not children, either. They know what they signed up for here. If we just stopped factoring in the way we feel about these people, Cree, and focused on their jobs—"

"They're not robots. You tried that. They—"

"Oh, *fuck off.*"

Cree quieted.

Dare made a harsh noise under his breath, telling Penny, "We didn't do nearly enough homework on what we were dealing with—had we done so before sending you to New York on a last-minute wild goose chase, then we would have seen what they didn't want us to. That they were using the same tactics we did to draw them out. It's not a mistake we'll make again. Any side trips after this will *not* be happening."

Penny didn't blink. "Fine. What about the rest of The Elite?"

"Renzo passed along the information about that side of things, I assume?"

"A little," she said. "I want to hear the rest from you."

"They're working with what they have. Which just changed into a whole lot more than we might be able to handle."

"And what does that—"

Dare reached over and tapped a key on his laptop, silencing Penny instantly when the screens switched from security camera views to something else entirely. The pyramid made up of faces had changed since the first time she saw it. Now, a few of the faces were grayed out with a large, red X crossing over their images.

Men …

Women.

All her victims.

Five years worth of her life stared at her from the glowing wall. Five years of hard work and pain to X out the few she had managed to end. After training that could only be described as complete and total hell, *years* overseas dismantling one organization kill by kill … she had finally come back home.

Here.

To get all of them.

The faces of The Elite watched her without movement or emotion. Yet, despite only being digital photographs, their presence and lives were still all too real to her. Especially the two pictures at the very top.

Neither had an X.

She hated that the most.

Unable to look away from the top two images—the people who controlled the innermost aspects of the pedophile ring—Penny ignored the sinking sensation in her stomach. *That* wasn't real, she had to tell herself. They no longer had the power to hurt her but especially not their images. She refused to even think their names.

"After a discussion with your boss," Dare said, "we've decided that it would be the right choice to call off any further hits on The Elite until we have a better idea of what we're dealing with."

Stay calm.

Maintain composure.

She didn't look away from the screens.

Couldn't.

Still …

"Why, because they're fighting back now?" she demanded. "Sounds like we just need to ramp up the pressure. If a little made them crack, then a lot will make them break."

"We need a safe route from—"

Penny scoffed, her sharp gaze finally cutting to Dare and breaking the haze she'd been in while staring at the screen. "*Nothing* about this was ever safe. We knew the risks. *I* know the risks and agreed anyway. It was the only way. You don't get to decide when the risks become too much for *me* to take, Dare. It's my choice."

"Actually, it's not. You didn't pay for your training and position. You don't make the final calls on the plans. You have a boss—"

"If we give them even a month to recoup, then it'll be like starting over!"

They had too much money.

Way too much power.

It would be stupid to let The Elite have even a second to start digging backward toward Penny and The League. They already had the bone; now they were just looking for the rest of the skeleton.

"I agree," Dare said calmly, "but in the last day, circumstances have changed and we have to consider what it means."

"I don't—"

"I know, Penny. You know nothing. You've been unplugged and underground, and then on a plane. I don't expect you to already *know*, just understand."

Dare hit another key on the laptop. The screens changed again to a news anchor sitting behind a desk ready to report—something Penny hadn't expected. What did this have anything to do with their current situation?

She would soon learn.

An image of a New Jersey senator flashed on the screen and the woman behind the desk smiled behind her painted mask of television makeup. "*Senator Gilles Tracey has announced his engagement today. We were expecting a different announcement from the senator's team this week— something like a presidential run in the upcoming election—but we were assured that was still on the table.*"

Penny blinked.

The image changed.

Her throat *closed*.

Two little girls—the caption said their names were Jennifer and Jules, twelve and ten years old respectively—stood in front of their father, the senator, and another woman. A familiar face. The same face Penny had been staring at for minutes without being able to look away just moments before when the pyramid of Elite members had been plastered across the screen.

"*Senator Tracey provided little details about the engagement but stated he planned to marry Allegra Hatheway within the next few months in a private ceremony.*"

She was different, now.

Her last name had changed. The white-blonde hair was now a caramel wave that fell over her shoulders in soft curls. She still looked entirely fit for her position as a trophy wife standing beside a rich and powerful man.

"Do you want me to let it keep—"

"Shut it off," Penny said through clenched teeth.

Dare did.

Beside her, Cree reached over to clasp her shoulder in his large palm. She side-stepped the touch, not wanting *anyone* too close. He didn't seem offended, but he did pass Dare a knowing glance.

"The report continues," Dare said softly. "It glosses over her previous husband and life. Probably because a lot of that happened years ago, and the senator has more money than he knows what to do with. I'm sure he doesn't want his future wife's dead husband's misdeeds staining his family's pristine reputation or ruining his potential run at the presidency when—"

"Is he in any way connected to *anything* we've gathered around The Elite?" she asked.

"It appears not."

But he had two girls.

That woman had access to two girls.

The screen switched back to the image of the pyramid and faces when the video player eventually minimized itself like it did when videos were paused for too long. Penny would have preferred to keep staring at the reporter doing her job than the face of a woman that had haunted her every waking moment since the first memories of her life. Every monster that had ever done her harm came from the permission of *that* woman.

Allegra Hatheway was Allegra Dunsworth.

Penny's mother.

Her image sat at the top of the pyramid alongside a man that had been an accomplice in her abuse and trafficking for years with her mother and father—her grandfather. Allegra's father. The whole family tree was rotten, and it started in the fucking *roots*.

She could still hear Dare talking—trying to explain things. It all felt like she was underwater, and everything was muffled around her.

"This is going to be a lot more difficult and messier with Allegra coming back to the spotlight in this way," Dare said from where he had moved to sit behind his desk. "It is possible that this move was purposeful; maybe even meant to hold off what's been happening to members of The Elite, but we're not really—"

"I need a minute."

Her words came out short.

Sharp.

Even to her own ears.

For a man who had been quick to say he needed to stop caring about the emotional needs of the people he controlled at The League, Dare didn't hesitate to nod and say, "Whatever you want. Just know, Penny ..."

She had already turned to leave, and while walking away, she heard him say, "You're to do *nothing* right now—not until we know their next move. Since you brought that man with you, staying at the complex is off the table, but we can just as easily keep an eye on you at the hotel. Go ... there. I won't say home because I know that isn't what it is for you. Either way, go there and stay out of sight. *Do not* force my hand. This is for the best."

Right.

The best.

But all she could think about?

Those little girls.

19.

Luca

"WHY was every room locked until I found this one?" Luca asked the presence that had joined him in what he could only describe as a music room.

"Because this was where Dare wanted you," Penny said simply.

"What, like—"

"He controls the locks on every room door and corridor. If one was unlocked, it was because he left it that way purposefully to direct you to the place where he wanted you to be."

Huh.

The whole damn place gave him the fucking creeps, but he wouldn't say so out loud. Cameras watched him from every corner. He couldn't even remember the many dirt roads they had taken deep into the desert to arrive. All the doors were black. Some didn't even have handles to open them. He hadn't seen a single soul, but maybe that was purposeful. Locks were controlled by a man with a strange name hidden somewhere he couldn't see. What, were they in The Wizard of Oz or some shit?

At least, he liked the room he was currently in. That was one good thing. Instruments lined the walls. Everything and anything one could want to indulge their musical interests waited for the right hands to pick the instrument of their choice. At first, he considered the row of vintage guitars, but the piano at the far side called his name just because of the nostalgia he felt looking at it.

He was far from a pianist.

That was all his sister.

And Penny, too.

Still, he dared to play. Of course, the piano seemed a bit out of tune. To his ear, anyway. The small set of familiar tools that he found under the piano gave him something to do as he tuned the instrument for a while as he waited to be found.

He figured … how hard would it be? All they had to do was check the cameras.

Right.

Sitting at the piano bench, Luca played a few keys, letting his fingers dance over ivory. *Mary Had A Little Lamb* rang out into the room, making Penny laugh.

"You missed a key," she noted. "And it's better in the higher note, I think."

Luca shrugged as she came to join him on the bench. He shot her a smile while he played the next few keys of the song. "Never said I was a pro."

Far from it.

"That was always Roz's thing," he added about his sister. "And I was just there to help or annoy her when she needed it."

"I don't think she needed the annoyance part."

"And you clearly never had a younger brother."

It was par for the course.

Basically siblings' rights.

His joke went over Penny's head when he glanced her way. The song came to a stop when he realized she wasn't smiling or even looking at him. Her stare had focused on the wall behind the piano, emotionless and dead. It was impossible to miss.

"What's wrong?"

"Nothing," Penny murmured, a fake smile tugging at the edges of her lips.

"You're a terrible liar."

"I'm a fantastic liar."

"Hard to argue with *that*."

Penny's hands lifted like she was considering playing the piano, but stopped short of resting on the keys when she said, "You know, Roz was more of a mother to me in the time I spent with her than my own ever was for my entire life."

This was not the conversation he expected. Especially not when she was supposed to be here for a briefing on her work. He didn't think she would share that information with him, either, but he wondered why she had Roz on her mind. Particularly in a mothering sense.

He wasn't going to pass the opportunity up to once again remind Penny that the woman she cared about enough to consider a mother still loved her and worried every day. *Like a mother would.*

"She still talks about you," Luca said, letting his fingers zip down half the keys in the span of a second, the twang annoying even to his own ears. "Sometimes, she'll be in random conversation and something reminds her of you … it's like she can't help herself. You're always on her mind. Those photos she took when you lived there? She hung them up with the family photos she had done with Naz and little Cross, too. You're still there even if you're *not*."

"I wish you wouldn't do that."

Luca nodded. "I know."

"Do you, *really*? Do you know how it aches inside my chest when you tell me that people I only wanted to help are hurting because—"

"That's why I keep telling you," he interjected, not unkindly even if he could plainly see her pain staring back at him from ice-blue eyes. "Because maybe if I do it enough, you'll let me go back and tell them you're okay. Even that would be better than what they have now, Penny. I'm only here because they want to know why."

"It's not occurred to you even once, has it?"

"What?"

Penny stood from the bench, muttering, "That I'm only here *because* they loved me, Luca. I don't need you to tell me things I already know." She didn't give him time to dissect those words. With a wave as she headed for the door, she told him, "Let's go. It's time to leave before someone changes their mind, and your bed tonight ends up being at the bottom of a hole somewhere."

Well ...

Okay, then.

• • •

Penny didn't have a home.

She had a *hotel.*

A suite—a nice one, mind—that felt nothing like her. It was the first thing he noticed when she slid the card through the lock and opened the door. There wasn't anything that suggested she had been here before, recently left, or even planned to return. Sure, the sitting room and small kitchenette were meticulously cared for and clean. The walls had a few scattered pieces of art that matched the decor. Likely compliments of the hotel.

But the place felt ...

Sterile.

Cold, even.

Penny must have noticed his curious stare sweeping the place because she was quick to say, "It does what I need it to, that's what counts."

"Which is?"

"A place to sleep."

Was that all she needed?

Just a place to *sleep?*

Hell, people did that on the fucking streets. Not by choice in most cases, he knew, but still ... if all she wanted was somewhere to lay her head at night, then he was sure there were cheaper or closer alternatives to the complex that had taken them over an *hour* to drive to once they hit the dry desert land.

At least the view was decent. He took the chance to admire the sight of the Vegas strip lit up down below as he followed behind Penny without a word. She hadn't suggested he should chase after her, but he also wasn't going to give her the choice at the moment.

Up until then, Luca had been fine to play whatever game she had going on between the two of them. If doing so meant gaining more information on her *and* possibly being able to bring her home, then what did it hurt?

She called the shots.

He let her.

But the missed calls and piling texts on his phone that she *hadn't* destroyed were starting to burn a hole in the back of his mind. Not that he'd answered any of them despite the growing frustration from Nazio's messages and his mother's constant stream of worries. Luca had been off the grid—unreachable by his family, friends, and even people who had jobs waiting on his back burner—for longer than he could excuse.

At this point, he was just playing with fire.

Inside a bedroom, Luca lingered by the doorway as Penny carelessly shed her clothing and tossed it to a nearby chair. She disappeared into the connected walk-in closet as he considered how to broach the fact that she was running out of time to make the choice of returning herself.

Not that he could *force* her to go back. The time for that had obviously passed long ago. He missed his chance there big time.

Luca knew that.

He wasn't stupid.

There were other means at his disposal, now. Ways he could expose her current life and location to the people who wanted that information. Except he was quite aware that could be dangerous for her. Someone had tried to kill her. How long would the Donatis have Penny on their radar—just to know she was alive and well—before the news was passed on to someone else who only meant to do her harm?

It made him pause.

Fucked his plans entirely.

Stuck between a rock and a hard place, Luca didn't know where to begin with his next move. He wondered …

"Was that your plan?" His question came out quiet when Penny reappeared from within the closet with an item that she dumped to the bed. "Get me close, let me see just enough of your business right now that I have a basic understanding of the situation you're in, and let me draw conclusions myself from there," he clarified at her silent stare. "Because why else would you stay put with me for days, right? Why else bring me here, too? The devil you know is better than the one you don't, huh?"

"Luca—"

"I think some of this was … all accidental."

"Some of it," she admitted. "*Most* of it."

"You're being hunted, aren't you?"

Penny didn't flinch.

In fact, she *smiled*.

"It was bound to happen, Luca. One can only keep the company of monsters for so long before they start to notice you're not quite the same."

Appropriate, he thought.

Considering everything ...

"You just had to go and make yourself a very *present* complication while it happened," she told him without any heat in her tone.

"And if I don't go along with keeping everything I know about you under the radar—"

"You already have your answer, I'm sure."

He did.

And it pissed him off.

Because he *understood*, too.

"I didn't plan very much," Penny added, shrugging as she opened a leather satchel across the bed. The spread of sharp knives in all shapes and sizes stared back, nestled in their hooks and glinting under the light of the bedside lamp. "I just let what was going to happen ... *happen*. Inevitable, you know?"

"No, I *don't*—"

"You're mad because I gave you what you wanted?"

Luca's brow lifted high. "*What?*"

"Access. You have access. *To me*. The thing you've been chasing for years. A ghost you couldn't catch but saw around every corner. I gave you what you wanted, and you're *mad* about it?"

"Are you fucking serious?"

"Ask me when I joke, Luca."

Man.

This female was something else.

Penny gave him one last look—it burned more than he wanted to admit—before she headed for the closet again. The next time she reappeared, she was punching her arms through a too-large T-shirt with a faded logo across the chest that barely covered the black cotton panties stretched over her pert ass.

Of course, his cock noticed those things.

Why wouldn't it?

It wasn't the fucking time.

"So, this is it?" he demanded.

Penny didn't reply.

He was getting really tired of that shit, too. Her silence. The lack of cooperation. He was fine and good to follow along like a puppy at her bidding but that was it. Any plans that related to her or that fucking place back in the desert were off the table entirely.

"Is this it, Penny? I can be here, but I can't *help* or know what's going on ... or do anything even remotely useful because—"

His words cut off when an item flew past his head with blinding speed. He didn't need to turn to see where the knife had embedded itself into the wood of the doorway. The corner of his eye provided that view just fine. She had picked that knife up and threw it with such precision that there had been no hesitation between her first move and the last. If she had meant for that blade to be buried in his chest, then that's exactly where it would have landed.

No lie, he swallowed a little bit harder in those few seconds when her gaze met his.

"*Remember*," she said, each word after a warning that he heard loud and clear, "you are here because I allowed it. That doesn't mean I owe you anything during or *after*."

He hit a nerve.

That much was clear.

But which one?

Luca searched for the reason, wracking his brain but all he could come up with was ... "Because I suggested I might be able to help? Or that you *won't* let me help."

"Just drop it."

"Penny, come on."

What was her aversion to talking?

It drove him *crazy*.

"Did you get those knives out just to throw one at me?"

"No, I wanted this one to peel the wax off the wine I've been saving." She didn't give him the chance to push the topic before she headed right for him, stopping at his side only long enough to yank the knife from the doorframe. The tip of the blade teased far too close to his chin when she said, "And now I need a damn drink, but I doubt the wine is going to be enough."

"Penny—"

"*Drop it.*"

"I didn't mean that you *needed* my help."

Wasn't that obvious?

The girl was a created killer. That place—those people—she worked for ... they had turned her into someone he was still trying to learn. She was a shell of who she used to be, but he no longer thought that was a bad thing.

That didn't mean she *liked* it.

Luca knew that.

He could have left Penny alone. That might have been the smarter option. Considering she *had* just thrown a knife at him. One she still had within reach. Instead, he followed her like a dumbass and watched from behind a couch as she poured herself a glass of whiskey at the wet bar facing the floor-to-ceiling windows overlooking the strip.

Her silence irked him.

More than he could explain.

Even as she lifted the glass of whiskey and swallowed two fingers worth of burning liquor without as much as a cringe, the feeling only festered inside of Luca. More and more. Until he was brimming with it and unwilling to keep quiet any longer.

How would that help?

Didn't she realize at all ...

"I fucking care," he told her. "Don't you get that? I *care*. That's all."

She wouldn't look at him.

Not even once.

"*Penny.*"

"*I know!*"

Her shriek exploded the same way the glass did when she slammed it against the marble top of the wet bar. Shards flew in every direction, one slicing the side of her hand while others tinkled as they bounced to the floor. Luca held back from rushing to help, but only because she pointed that bloody hand at him like she didn't want him anywhere near her.

Even when she was in pain.

"I know that," she said, an ache coating her every word. "I'm not that out of touch, Luca. I have a *heart*. And a soul, too, despite everyone who tried to sell it. Do you really think I don't know that's why you've done all of this? Why you tracked me for all this time—why you're willing to *be* here right now, lying to the people you love, *for me*? Yes, I know!"

That was it, he knew.

It hit him like a brick to the chest.

"Because you do, too. Care," he clarified, seeing how she fought to maintain some semblance of control even as she yanked the splinter of glass from her hand without a flinch. Her hands shook, like her shoulders and her bottom lip. She fought back tears while forcing her expression to remain stone-like. "About everyone you left behind. About the kids you're trying to help by doing what you're doing. *Me*. You care about—"

"Just ... *fuck off*," she snapped.

"No."

He took one step toward her.

She shook her head. "You need to stop."

"Tell me that. Tell me *exactly* what you want me to do, Penny. Tell me no or tell me you hate me. Tell me you're never coming back—that everything I've done up until now is pointless because the life you left behind is no longer yours."

He didn't stop until he was right in front of her. Until their chests touched, her wrists, even the one with blood still dribbling down in a morbid trail, was locked in his hands, and he had her backed into the window.

"Go ahead," he murmured, tipping his head down so her eyes were locked with his. "Tell me. I'll wait."

"Fuck you."

"That's not a real *answer*." He let go of her wrists, ready to fend off a slap or worse, but they only dropped loosely to her sides. His palms found her face, and he closed the inch left between them so she understood. It was him and her in that second. Two fucking humans with hearts and feelings and thoughts of their own. "I don't want the programmed shit you've been feeding people—or they've been feeding you—for years. All that's ever done is kept people from knowing you were *hurting*. You can put up walls and protect yourself from the world ... but not from me. You never needed to, remember? I told you once."

"Luca, *please* ... I'm begging you to just leave it—"

"I'm safe for you. Whatever kind of safe you need, Penny. *Then,* and now."

"*I like this. I hate that I like this.*"

The words escaped from her in a hiss those clenched, perfect teeth that her pretty lips had parted to show him just how much the truth hurt. Clear tears had tracked lines over her near-translucent skin, finally escaping despite the fight she'd put up to keep them hidden. The wetness stopped at his hands that were still holding tighter to her face than they should. She didn't shy away, though.

Not from his touch.

Or him.

That static anger snapping between them, and the fact they both gave a shit enough to be standing there doing it at all. And that's what she meant, he knew. He couldn't stop himself.

Not from saying what he already did, or even knowing that he'd finally pushed her to the edge, asking next, "You hate that you like me ... or whatever's this is—this *crazy shit*. How many people make you this angry? *Irrationally so.* How many people have touched you because you *wanted* them to the way I do? That's what you mean."

Her next words were not what he expected, ready for more denials or fight. Anything but the truth that kicked him straight in the goddamn heart and explained everything he needed to know in two sentences.

"I can't afford to let myself wonder what happens when I like this—*us,*" Penny said, shrugging weakly. "Life taught me not to."

This wasn't the kind of thing he could push. There were just parts of Penny's very psyche that even when she had every ounce of proof that she was fine and okay, her brain and heart didn't believe it was true. A learned *instinct*. One she would have to relearn—it was a process. It started with him, though. It began with the people who gave a shit repeating things she already knew just for the sake of *saying* it until it became the new reality.

The truth.

"I'm *safe*, Penny."

Whatever kind of safe she needed—person, place, or otherwise. He would keep saying it until she finally heard it. Even if right now wasn't the time when she did. It still needed to be said.

"I know," she whispered.

He was still angry.

Nothing was right. She hadn't answered anything or cleared up what was happening with her people or otherwise. He didn't know the plans—if there even were any. There were a million more questions he wanted to ask because he knew eventually, she would break and yet …

Luca kissed her, instead.

Why?

She looked like she needed it.

God knew so did he.

20.

Penny

A single kiss from Luca could change everything. The hard crush of his mouth against hers had the capability to sweep the world away. It was shocking to Penny how willing she was to let him do exactly that, too.

Because he wasn't wrong.

She *did* want him.

His hands tight on her body, grabbing and teasing and making her nerves sing. His taste hot in her mouth, bliss whispered in every grunt and moan. The weight of his body pressing against hers with nothing but skin between them. She *wanted* him.

Willingly.

Completely.

That terrified her.

But it was also easy.

Scarily so.

It was far too easy to slip into the need that coursed through her body with every slash of his tongue against hers. The chaotic rush of his hands to strip her of the over-sized T-shirt matched the demand of her own to get him naked, too.

Before she even understood what happened, her back pressed against the window. Cold glass kissed her bare ass. She shoved his pants down to let his cock spring free. He was already hard and hissing when she wrapped her fingers around the heavy girth of his length to stroke him until she could feel his pulsing in her palm.

Maybe they had talked enough. Or maybe he didn't know what else to say to try to tempt truths from Penny that she wasn't willing to give him. Either way, they were all out of words.

Their fight was different, now.

Still harsh.

Every touch ached.

She tasted his blood when her teeth caught his lip, but it only made him kiss her harder. The copper flavor washing over her tongue as his cussed *fuck* pounded against her mouth. And then he was lifting her to the window without warning.

Her fingernails found purchase in his strong shoulders, digging in for stability when the flex of his hips drove him home. Straight into heaven.

Bliss *could be* heaven, she knew.

With him.

She felt every glorious inch of him. How he filled her without a sense of hesitation. The sting was beautifully real while she tensed, and her sensitive tissues accommodated his size. The sharp lines of his face were all the more intense from the shadows casting over his features. Yet, it hid nothing.

Not the hunger.

The *want*...

Or the drive she found there.

She melted into him; from the kiss he stole to the way her thighs widened under his demanding hands. Her body gave into his torturous control, and the pleasure she knew would soon follow them both straight over the cliff into something wicked and *good.*

Luca had been right.

He *was* safe for her. Safe to trust that his hands wouldn't hurt even when they pinned her to the glass, so she couldn't move while he pounded into her. Her heart jumpstarted and stuttered when his mouth traveled from hers to the line of her jaw where he could lick and bite—but it didn't start in any kind of fear. And when he did finally start murmuring dirty promises and other sinful words that made her shake, there was no disgust pounding at her insides.

Every grunted *take that cock* and his breathy *you're loving this* made her hotter until she was ready to scream. He liked those sounds, too. Each whine and whisper. He licked every single one from her mouth the second it left her lips.

Nothing about him was wrong.

Or bad.

It was all *good* for her. Especially like this. Safe in a way not many people have ever afforded her. Not as easily as Luca did.

"You drive me *crazy,*" he panted against her parted lips, the flex of his hips slapping against hers at a pace that already had her spiraling. His hands held tighter like if he didn't, she might burst all apart. "There it is, yeah?"

All she could do was nod. The orgasm clutched at her throat as it ripped through her womb. There was something to be said about pleasure when it was raw; how it raked over every nerve almost violently, but it still felt *perfect.*

Like nothing else.

He'd not slowed under her orgasm began to wane and even then, he teased her body with long, languid strokes. She was wet enough to hear every drive of his cock into her sex, but it was the drag of his length along every tensing inner muscle that kept her live like a wire.

"You drive me *crazy,*" he told her.

The only thing Penny could think to say when Luca pulled her away from the window and bent her over the back of the couch was, "*We're both crazy.*"

He fucked her harder like that—with fingers tangled into her hair while his palm left behind red prints on her ass until the heat spread everywhere all over again.

For a time, she forgot everything. All of it. She didn't want reality to catch up, but it would ...

Soon.

It always did.

• • •

Penny should be sleeping, lost in dreamland while wrapped in the arms of a man she wasn't supposed to have. She should have appreciated the fact she could do that at all but instead, she was spiraling.

Not that Luca was aware.

Over the edge of her laptop, she could see him stretched out on his stomach where he slept without worry. He used one arm to bunch around a pillow, keeping it higher for his head, while his other rested limply across her side of the bed. Like maybe he knew she had gotten up after he fell asleep, and even in his slumber, he was trying to reach for her.

To pull her back.

He was constantly pulling her back.

Did he know that?

Did he know how it confused her?

It was a horrible feeling to both want something but know it could never be hers. That's exactly what Luca was for her. A piece of her past that she hadn't even asked for until it was laid at her feet, but there was no way she could keep him.

The white sheets pooled just below his waist, the curve of his backside teasing the fabric low enough that she could appreciate the sight of his body even in the darkness. Strong shoulders. A back still red with lines from her fingernails. Skin that she could still feel moving against hers if she dared to let her mind wander back that way.

But she couldn't.

Not now ...

Instead, she spiraled.

Behind the screen of a laptop, she fell even more into the rabbit hole of information in front of her. Anything she could find on her mother or the man Allegra was meant to marry, she absorbed each word like it might keep her alive. Already, she had worked her way through every article that had ever been published on the Jersey senator, his daughters, and even his wife that had died in a tragic car accident only a few years prior.

He *seemed* like a good man.

On paper, everyone did.

Penny knew that better than anyone.

The scars she hid beneath the sweats and hoodie she had thrown on after getting out of bed itched and burned. It started the second she dared to open her laptop and type in Allegra's new name, determined to find the proof that she needed.

The proof her mother hadn't changed. Monsters never did. They were who they were. Of course, she knew Allegra was the same bitch she had been when Penny was under her control ... the actions and business of The Elite was more than enough to tell her that.

But she had to know ...

Those little girls—were *they* next?

Were they Allegra's next *Penny*? The next *perfect* little girl to train and groom and sell to the highest bidder ... after bidder.

Because it wouldn't end.

Once it started, there was no stopping the lifelong horrors that followed. Even after Penny escaped through cutting and misbehavior that caused her parents to discard her to whatever private institution would take her, it still didn't fucking *end.* She felt it in every scar; lived with the pain in her mind that wasn't physical but affected her all the same.

Her memories lived on, too.

Crystal clear.

It didn't matter that her mother had been living under the radar since her deceased husband's arrest years ago and his subsequent murder behind bars. The woman hadn't stepped back from the pedophile ring her father— Penny's grandfather—had been running for decades. The sex trafficking business was lucrative one but especially when it came to the filthy rich where cost was no issue to feed their addictions and depravities.

Penny already had her answer; she didn't need to look for another sign to further prove what she believed to be true. Jules and Jennifer Tracey were in the mouth of a lion—only ten and twelve years old, how could they possibly know?

Did their father?

How could he *not?*

It made Penny angry. Drunk and pissed off wasn't a good combination for her—especially not when she was already dancing between the present and the past while she stared at the photo of her mother, the senator, and his two daughters on the laptop screen.

Underneath the photo was an article discussing the happy couple and their next plans. The announcement of an upcoming engagement dinner at a restaurant owned by the Tracey family in New York City.

Penny could end it ...

All of it.

She just needed the chance.

Scrolling back up the article to the photo, she stared at the monster looking back. Allegra smiled *her* smile. The one that blinded the world to the dangers and vile truths hiding behind her beauty. A smile she had turned on Penny like a weapon time and time again.

She couldn't *forget*.

She tried.

Sometimes, she was lucky enough to go days now without a memory or a dream that threw her back in time. The PTSD that once kept her locked in a constant haze of hell had lessened with training, purpose, and *life*.

But those things did nothing for her then. It didn't protect her from slipping into a memory of a six-year-old her that had finally started to learn what it meant when her mother smiled.

"Don't you want to make Daddy happy, Penny?"

Her mother smiled, her perfect white teeth matching the color of the dress that swished when she walked, her tall heels clicking against wood floors as she came closer. The rest of the world saw that smile and grinned back. Penny saw her mother's smile and shrunk away, knowing what it meant ...

"Stop your crying—good girls don't cry." Only a few feet away from where Penny sat on the edge of the piano bench, Allegra sighed where she stopped. "Are you going to wipe away those tears, or should I?"

Penny did it.

Pretty girls didn't cry, either.

"Now, are you about done?" Allegra asked.

"Yes," she whispered.

A promise she had to keep.

Even though she could barely stand to hold her knees together how she had been told to by her mother while she waited for her father to arrive for another lesson, she did it. She did everything she was told despite the constant pain that accompanied every movement and the dry spot of blood she had found in her panties that morning.

Because like her mother explained ...

A good girl was treated well.

But a pretty girl was treated even better.

Allegra clapped her hands together, her pleasure with Penny clear as she called over her shoulder, "Preston, we're ready to begin."

Penny came out of the memory with a gasping sob that caught in her throat. She barely managed to muffle the sound into her hand. But it took biting into the heel of her palm to keep the next one from coming out.

The sting was *everything*. An addictive sensation.

It took away the bad. Numbed. *Left her with nothing*. And nothing was better than the alternative.

The form on the bed shifted, but Luca didn't wake up. Penny's teeth didn't release the bite until her breaths had steadied. Her heart still raced out of control, though.

It was one memory in a million. One moment of too many ...

The very idea that another little girl—or *two*, as it were—might be put through the same hell Penny had lived with for years under the direction and control of her mother ... well, it was just too much to handle. A part of her felt fractured from that alone. Somehow, despite being battered into a billion pieces, parts of her remained that could still break.

Her orders from The League about this were clear. She understood *why*.

She also knew that if she did nothing, then she was complicit in someone else's pain. One she was far too familiar with and that no one deserved.

It was time to slay another monster. Even if it meant ruining everything for everyone else.

Penny no longer cared as she deposited her laptop to the chair after standing with her final decision cemented in her heart.

A *broken* heart.

She took one of the knives from the leather satchel she had left on the dresser and headed for the attached bathroom. For the first time in years, she cut—a single line that bled in droplets to the sink—but she didn't make a sound.

Not even when she dug two fingers into the bleeding wound in her upper arm to find the item there while agony tore through every fiber of her being. Instead, she focused all that pain into her reflection staring back from the mirror. A face that looked far too much like the woman who had done this to her in the first place.

How could she run from a monster that looked back at her everyday?

No one would understand why it had to happen like this. Not Luca, when he woke up tomorrow to find Penny gone. Certainly not her handlers when someone realized the chip in her arm—that now rested at the bottom of the bloody sink drain—hadn't showed any movement activity in hours. Not the team of people at The League who had been working with Penny for years so that their plan to dismantle and end The Elite could finally culminate to a successful job. One that would earn the organization millions from the man who delivered her *and* the job to them in the first place.

Not one of them would be able to justify anything she did. Because they weren't *her*. They didn't live inside her head or past the way she did. They couldn't go back in time like she was forced to all the time in her memories to explain why it all had to happen like this.

But she wasn't sorry.

She wouldn't apologize for this or leaving them behind to do what needed done. Something she should have finished years ago. Maybe when it was all over, the people who did matter would allow her the chance to ask for forgiveness.

One step after another, she thought. Each one she took led her right back to her mother.

Everything she did, before this and after, it was all one big circle that was destined to eventually return to the place it began. There was only one way it could stop. Wasn't it time for this to finally end?

It started with her mother.

Penny would end it there, too.

• • •

Want to continue Penny and Luca's story – grab *ONE BREATH AFTER ANOTHER* by visiting bethanykris.com/OneBreath!

ABOUT THE AUTHOR

Bethany-Kris is a Canadian author, lover of much, and mother to four sons, three cats, and four dogs. A small town in Eastern Canada where she was born and raised is where she has always called home. With her boys under her feet, a snuggling cat, barking dogs, and a spouse calling over his shoulder, she is nearly always writing something ... when she can find the time.

Find Bethany-Kris at her:

www.bethanykris.com

OTHER BOOKS

Andino + Haven

Duty
Vow
One Last Time
Andino + Haven: The Complete Duet

John + Siena

Loyalty
Disgrace
John + Siena: The Complete Duet
John + Siena: Extended

Cross + Catherine

Always
Revere
Unruly
The Companion
Naz & Roz

Guzzi Duet

Unraveled, Book One
Entangled, Book Two
Cara & Gian: The Complete Duet

DeLuca Duet

Waste of Worth: Part One
Worth of Waste: Part Two

Standalone Titles

Pink
Pretty Lies
Dirty Pool
Effortless
Inflict
Cozen
Captivated
Dishonored

Donati Bloodlines

Thin Lies
Thin Lines
Thin Lives
Behind the Bloodlines
The Complete Trilogy

Filthy Marcellos

Antony
Lucian
Giovanni
Dante
Legacy
A Very Marcello Christmas
The Complete Collection

Seasons of Betrayal

Where the Sun Hides
Where the Snow Falls
Where the Wind Whispers
Seasons: The Complete Seasons of Betrayal Series

Gun Moll Trilogy

Gun Moll
Gangster Moll
Madame Moll

The Chicago War

Deathless & Divided
Reckless & Ruined
Scarless & Sacred
Breathless & Bloodstained
The Complete Series
Maldives & Mistletoe

The Russian Guns

The Arrangement
The Life
The Score
Demyan & Ana
Shattered
The Jersey Vignettes

FANTASY ROMANCE

The Hunted: A 9INE REALMS Novel

Find more on Bethany-Kris's website at www.bethanykris.com.

www.ingramcontent.com/pod-product-compliance
Lightning Source LLC
Chambersburg PA
CBHW071439260626
47170CB00008B/2771